Prai

"Reading this exuberant collection of stories was a thrill! The premises are bold and original, funny and heartbreaking in equal measure. I love a writer who keeps me guessing, who refuses to pull their punches, and Brankin delivers time and time again. The table of contents alone is worth the price of admission."

– Gwen E. Kirby, author of *Shit Cassandra Saw*

"*Attention Seekers* is full of masterful stories. At times darkly funny, sad, and irreverent, there's something for everyone in this collection. I can't remember the last time I was held so deeply by a book – these stories linger long after reading them. Emma Brankin has established herself as a force in the literary world. I'd read anything by her."

– Morgan Talty, author of *Night of the Living Rez*

"Dark humour meets scathing social observations in this fantastic new collection. *Attention Seekers* deconstructs what it means to be a modern woman, and lays the seediest, most shameful parts of our souls on display; fans of Eliza Clark and Emma Jane Unsworth will especially relish Brankin's unreliable, selfish, and vengeful narrators. The collection not only kicks down the pedestal women are expected to delicately perch on, but sets it fully ablaze."

– Lindz Mcleod, author of *Turducken*

"Brankin's stories delight and surprise with their audacity and coruscating wit. A rising star."

– Tom Vowler, author of *The Method*

"*Attention Seekers* is a hilarious, irreverent, and ultimately heartbreaking collection that examines what it means to be human in an online world. [...] Brankin takes chances and pushes boundaries, daring us to look away from the ensuing wreckage of these rich stories, skilfully confident in the knowledge that she holds our attention fast."
– Sara Hills, author of *The Evolution of Birds,* winner of Best Short Story Collection at the Saboteur Awards

"There's so much to enjoy in this mordant, affecting, highly inventive collection. Emma Brankin has a keen eye and a sharp wit, and her stories will resonate with anyone out there who's caught up in the current struggle to be a real person rather than a screen."
– Richard Kelly, author of *The Knives*

"Emma's story, 'The Scandals of Christendom', stood out for its imagination, character, beauty and the protagonist's life force."
– Eloghosa Osunde, author of *Vagabonds!* (shortlisted for the Waterstones Debut Fiction Prize) in selecting Emma's writing for the 2021 Fugue Fiction Prize

"I so enjoyed Brankin's selection of stories. A complex assortment of characters [are] cleverly rendered in this intriguing collection."
– Heather Darwent, author of *The Things We Do To Our Friends*

"Brilliant, brilliant stories."
– Nell Stevens, author of *Briefly, A Delicious Life*

Attention Seekers

Emma Brankin

Valley Press

First published in 2023 by Valley Press
Woodend, The Crescent, Scarborough, YO11 2PW
www.valleypressuk.com

ISBN 978-1-915606-28-0
Cat. no. VP0219

A CIP record for this book is available from the British Library.

Cover illustration by Myriam Létourneau.
Cover and text design by Jamie McGarry.
Editing by Jo Haywood.

Contents

for Sabre

'The secret to life is to put yourself in the right lighting. For some, it's a Broadway spotlight, for others a lamplit desk.'

– Susan Cain, *Quiet*

'I Googled myself recently – without lubricant. I don't recommend it.'

– Carrie Fisher, *The Late Show with David Letterman*

Caturday

The cat surpasses Ash in Instagram followers. She tells herself she doesn't mind, but she does. Gone is that flighty fluttering of validation in her chest whenever her phone buzzes. Now, the likes, comments, and follows are almost never for her. Even the most recent post – of the cat's tail – is proving infuriatingly popular.

She sighs. Over on her personal account, there is an underwhelming response to her most recent upload. Thirty-four likes. The cat could get that many likes just coughing up a photo of a furball.

She types 'Jenna' into her search bar. As the profile loads, air jams in her chest but the same sight greets her: Blocked.

The cat enters the living room. Ash reaches out a welcoming hand but its eyes narrow as it looks away. This is nothing new. The cat, despite being unaware of its burgeoning celebrity status, has always had the ego and entitlement of a Kardashian. The animal dumps its black, furry backside onto the carpet, unfurls a leg like a pole dancer and, with a Barbie-pink tongue, begins licking its crotch.

Her phone buzzes with comments about the tail:

SooOOooOOoo fluffy.

Swish swish bish.

Feather boa fierceness.

Ash scowls. She's cultivated a charming online presence for the cat, but, like a stage-mother, lip curling while clutching a vodka martini in the wings, she's growing to resent her ungrateful offspring.

She bats one of the cat's toys towards it. The animal watches

as the ball travels beyond its reach. Its uninterest is palpable. Then, for reasons only known to itself, it decides to chirrup, twist onto its back and writhe shamelessly. Ash dutifully switches on her phone's camera and starts snapping. She then spends the next thirty minutes deciding which filter best accentuates the animal's emerald-flecked eyes.

Then, something incredible happens. Dazed, she holds out her phone as if to show the cat her screen. She reads the notification aloud, every word soaked in incredulity.

'Jenna has liked your image.'

It appears Ash's ex has chosen to keep in contact with the cat.

Jenna likes five more pictures on the cat's account over the next few days. Ash screen-grabs everything and conducts hourly social media autopsies about what it all might mean. She obsesses forensically over the nature of the photos her ex singles out, the times of day the interactions occur, the rate of her liking. Ash's uploads become more frequent. Captions more pointed. She plants objects in the background to send Jenna subliminal messages, reminders of happier, relationship-filled times. Posts with the cat in front of the television watching their favourite programme. The cat curled up on top of the jumper Jenna left behind. The cat snoozing in the bathroom sink, with Ash's reflection, face fully made up, clearly visible in the mirror above it. She posts a heartstring-plucking throwback to the day they brought the cat home, this wiry blip of a creature resting on Jenna's lap. Her ex instantly adored the cat, cooing over its every paw-stretch and nose twitch. Suddenly, Jenna, who had considered being a 'social media sceptic' a core tenet of her personality, was now asking: 'Can you hashtag Caturday if it's not Saturday?'; 'Which string chase video should I upload?';

'What's a good caption for a cat wearing sunglasses?'

Ash spends hours every day poring over pictures of the three of them scattered in the depths of her account. Her finger hovers over, but cannot press down on, delete.

To distract herself from further obsessing, Ash tries to make plans with friends but every near-arrangement unravels. In a misguided attempt to remind people she exists, she uploads a photograph to her own account of her dinner and promptly loses nine followers. Meanwhile, the cat receives an invitation to a 'VIP pamper spa' sponsored by a pet food company. Faced with the horror of the cat's social life eclipsing hers, Ash agrees to a meal out with her mother.

It is there, three red wines deep – having endured lengthy updates about her father's ear wax appointments – that her mother finally broaches her most pressing concern, namely, Ash's abject loneliness and plummeting self-confidence.

'You still seem very sad, my Asheni. What about meeting somebody at an evening class? Shiv met her husband on a spoon carving course.'

'That's not necessary, Mum.' Ash pours herself a fourth glass of wine.

'What does that mean? Are you seeing someone?'

She feels her phone, sitting on her lap, glow with secrets.

'No…'

'Well?'

Ash takes a contemplative glug of wine. She knows her mother won't understand the technological intricacies of her current situation. She'll just wind up stuck in another conversation about social media where she has to explain what a belfie is.

'I don't know… I guess, I think Jenna is… maybe… regretting how she handled things.' She can't quite tuck

away the small smile forming.

'She's been in touch? After all these months of silence?'

'No, not quite. Well… it's hard to… Yes.' To hide her gleaming eyes, Ash picks up her phone. She flicks over to the cat's account and auto-pilot types 'Jenna'.

'Be careful, my Asheni.' Her mother's lips purse in a fruitless effort to keep her opinions to herself. 'That girl cut things off with you after all those years together with no explanation or apology. Leaving you with that unsanitary, undisciplined animal to look after all on your own.'

Ash's mother has never forgiven the cat for clawing a hole in her best cashmere jumper.

'Mum…'

'I'm just saying. Did Jenna offer to continue paying for vet bills?'

'No.'

'Or…' She sticks her fork into her salad with as much micro-aggression as she can muster, 'pay for a new sweater?'

Ash scrolls through her phone again to discourage the brewing rant. Then, she sees something. Her eyes flick from screen to mother to screen again. She forces her smile to stay set, tightening it until her skin hurts. Eventually, she excuses herself to go to the bathroom, sits down in a cubicle and stares, unblinking, at her phone screen.

She sees: Jenna laughing in a bar, wearing her tight green halter top, her hair in messy waves. She's not alone. There's a woman next to her, a redhead whose eyes are confidently – no, confrontationally – fixed on the camera and whose smile is lopsided, satisfied, smug. Ash focuses on their hands, which rest casually side by side, Jenna's index finger twisting around the woman's thumb. There's no caption. No hashtag. Just a photo that, like that index finger, twists once, cleanly, into the wound.

Ash's return home interrupts the cat's evening of solitude. She pours herself another drink then collapses onto the sofa, pulling the pet onto her lap.

'Come here and need me.'

The animal relents to Ash's adoration while, with her non-petting hand, she refreshes her phone's different accounts. Thoughts thump against one another: Jenna and the red-headed woman; cat photo after cat photo; liked, not liked; still blocked; the sight of their hands resting together with such ease. Her head feels heavier by the second, her strokes of the cat becoming robotic, like a conveyer belt of affection.

She scours Jenna's online footprint: two new LinkedIn connections and she's – finally – deleted her Iggy Azalea playlist on Spotify. But nothing indicates a change that would result in this new Jenna. In the devoted, funny, kind Jenna she knew twisting and morphing into this. A Jenna capable of such a cold, clinical severing of two lives. Ash chews the side of her mouth and a tear, polluted with eyeliner, tracks down her face. She feels conned. The relationship Ash had been enjoying, Jenna must have been enduring. Wiping her face with her sleeve, she downs the dregs of her drink while flicking through pictures of herself she took in the taxi home. She mistakes her glazed, drunken eyes for sultry and alluring and considers posting an image on her account but then pauses. She doesn't want to risk another depressive episode. She's only just recovered from the time a picture of the cat yawning got more likes than her birthday selfie.

Ash looks around her living room. Memories of Jenna fill every space in what was once their home. They linger, like phantoms, watching her cheerlessly, fascinated by her devotion to misery. Ash could have met a nice girl on Tinder.

Instead, she respected the relationship's demise by wallowing. But not Jenna. She had the audacity to move on with her life.

Phone in hand and alcohol in bloodstream, Ash misidentifies her indignation and anger as decisiveness and rationality. She uploads the pouting picture of herself to the cat's account, captioning the photo: 'Thinking about dyeing my hair RED.' Then, she sits, wholly satisfied with her unsubtle use of capitalisation, her drunkenness drowning any shame. Eventually, her phone vibrates.

'You really need to grow up, Ash.'

Jenna's message propels her out of her seat. She plants a hand on the cat, as if to steady the animal's emotions rather than her own.

'Oops. Accidentally posted to the cat's account by mistake. How u?' She types furiously, rushing into the kitchen to pour herself another drink, clamping the cat under her arm, its impassive emotional support essential to her well-being. The icon flicks, showing that her message has been read. Three minutes pass. Her drink finished, she drills her fingers against the kitchen counter, running through her options. She types again. 'This is the cat asking btw lol.'

Nothing.

'I don't know what your message means, Jen. I'm just a bit drunk looool.' A pause as she thinks. 'Nice to hear from you though.'

Nothing. She fills her drink again.

'Wine emoji, smiley face emoji, hands in face emoji.'

Nothing. She downs another. In the reflective curve of the kettle, she glimpses a sad, misshapen clown with smeared eye-makeup.

'I'm only asking as a friend.'

Still silence. Ash fires off a series of messages without

waiting for a response.

'I don't understand why you contact me and then don't reply?'

'So doooo you think I should dye my hair red?'

'Are u out?'

'I'm gonna do it!'

'I'm running the shower, about to dye it unless you say no.'

'Guess you must prefer me as a redhead then. WONDER why.'

'Joke!!!'

'Always hard to tell if jokes come across on text.'

'Do you think the red hair dye would work on black cat hair hahahahaha?'

Her phone finally buzzes.

'I can't believe I'm actually having to message you this,' Jenna types. 'But just in case you're THAT drunk… don't dye the cat's fur red.'

The last thing Ash remembers is dancing around the kitchen, holding her phone tightly, and the cat sitting on the counter, paws tucked under its body, watching her with its judgemental green eyes.

The next morning, head pounding, Ash lays in bed as the cat purrs at her feet. She can't stop rereading her exchange with Jenna. The exchange that happened *after* she blacked out.

'Sorry, I've not been myself these last few days after some bad news,' the message from Ash to Jenna at 11.58pm reads.

'What's wrong?'

12.03am: 'The cat's sick.'

Ash shakes her head. Her drunken, desperate brain had discovered the key to keeping her ex's attention: the cat. It was what Jenna missed the most.

12.09am: 'Been to endless vet appointments – it's the kidneys. They are doing everything they can. It's been really tough. I hadn't planned on saying anything. You seemed determined to cut communication. But you've caught me at an emotional moment. Sorry.'

Ash groans.

'Oh my god. I'm so sorry you're having to go through this, Ash. I love that little fur goblin. Stay positive x'

Jenna's 'x' provides a small reprieve from the toxic cocktail of anxiety and guilt sludging through Ash's hungover body. It makes her smile to imagine Jenna pressing down on the 'x', imbuing it with her compassion, support and love.

Five days pass and no further communication is initiated. Ash feels the weight of her empty flat, lonely evenings and quiet phone all the more. Paranoid that Jenna has rumbled her lies, she stops letting the cat out unsupervised, beckons it away from sunbathing by the window and, desperate to keep up the ruse, Googles cat-sized neck cones.

Things get worse when she hunts for information about Jenna's mystery redhead. She discovers: her name is Imogen; she's a lacrosse player with infuriatingly nice thighs; a brands manager; an aunty; a *dog* owner. Imogen has a worrying amount of Jenna content on her profiles, though the captions and hashtags never explicitly clarify their relationship. This frustrates Ash, who is willing to fully unravel, if only the world would give a full-strength tug. Then, she finds a tagged post revealing Imogen is currently attending a birthday party in a pub twenty minutes away. Surely, Jenna must be there with her.

Before Ash knows it, she's walking down the street, unable to explain what is propelling her forward, other than a desire to be hurt, to be wronged, to replace the emptiness

with something tangible – if that has to be pain and worthlessness, then so be it.

At the pub, she sees her – Imogen, not Jenna – in the garden with friends. Her whole body braces. Petrified, she stands still, pretending she's sending messages on her phone as she listens to snatches of their conversation. They laugh about: nights out, work mix-ups, things they've watched on telly. For a moment, Ash forgets about Jenna. Instead, she imagines sliding through the gaps between their bodies and letting the ease of their conversation, their togetherness, fill her up until she floats.

'Excuse me, do you have a light?'

Ash snaps to attention to find the woman next to Imogen looking at her. She fumbles around in her jacket for a long time – too long – before remembering she's never smoked a day in her life.

'Uh, sorry… no.'

For a second, she catches Imogen's expression: bemused, sceptical, assured. Somebody laughs and Ash flushes pink, trying to blink away the guilt carved into her face. She turns away, walking back out into the street. By the time she gets to the end of the road, she is already checking her phone. 'Jenna was last online two hours ago.' She looks at her Instagram account – down three followers today. The cat has twenty-seven new followers plus a never-ending stream of likes and comments. She rereads her messages to Jenna. 'The cat is sick.' The possibility that Imogen might have recognised her makes her chest screw unbearably tight and then tighter still. She thinks about how the group of women looked at her as she stood there, alone and uncertain. Ash starts typing Jenna a message then stops herself and tries to be calm and centred. To breathe deeply. But, before she knows it, she's flicking through potential new cat photos to post.

Slumping down onto a wall, she smacks the palms of her hands against her temple as if that might stop the relentless, multiple ways her mind keeps betraying her. A new thought zips through. If she is capable of stalking, of lying, of obsessing, then perhaps she needs to use these skills to help *herself* out for once. She sits for a long time, looking out into the dark, empty night. The buzz of voices from the pub grows more distant, as if she's quashing and sealing them away.

She makes her decision, taps away at her keys, then presses upload.

Her new post shows: a close-up of the cat, its green eyes quizzical, its black fur framing its face like a lion's mane. Underneath: 'RIP to my furry love. 2016 – 2020.'

In her bathroom mirror, Ash adopts a sombre, serious expression. She slaps her cheeks as if to relax them but remains unhappy with her reflection. She still looks significantly more guilty than grief stricken.

Ash tried to stop today's visit from happening but Jenna was insistent. 'I want to be there for the burial.' The burial of a cat that, a few hours ago, was deposited – very much alive – at Ash's dismayed mother's house.

Her phone has not stopped vibrating with grief since she posted the message. In between navigating the constant waves of shame, Ash spends most of her time reading heartfelt tributes from strangers who never met the cat.

Rest In Purrs, fluffy one.

My rainbow bridge baby will share his treats with you in heaven.

Life is so cruel – my stick insect's been alive longer.

Her own friends send banal condolences. One even offers to sell Ash their guinea pig.

Her buzzer goes a few minutes earlier than expected. Before letting Jenna in, she walks gravely to the hall cupboard, tips her hoover upside down and empties the dust into an old shoebox. She sighs. It's a sorry end, not for the cat, but for the last speck of dignity Ash has left.

She waits in the hallway, holding the box rigidly. When Jenna walks through the door, there is a long silence. Ash notices the half-filled cat food bowl is still out and nudges it out of sight with her foot. Jenna walks past her into the living room, which is filled with vast arrays of flowers sent by various online pet companies. She sinks into an armchair, hugging her knees with a distant, tortured look in her eyes. Ash hovers by the door, too nauseous to appreciate the much-desired sight of Jenna back in their home. She waits for her ex to speak.

'The place seems… different.'

'It's not.'

'You've not done something?'

'No.'

'It seems more… airy and light.'

'Oh.'

'That painting's new?'

'Oh. Yeah, that's new.'

'Feels weird without…'

'Yeah.'

Jenna's eyes fill with tears so Ash tries to change the subject.

'So, what's your new place like?'

'I'm not sure if we should talk about things like that.'

'Right…'

They endure further silence.

'What do you want to – '

An explosion of noise bursts out of Jenna, making Ash –

and her box of vacuum dust – jump. She is weeping. Loudly. And snottily. Ash sits down and reaches out her hand to pat her ex's back. It feels uncomfortable, as if her muscles are moving in an awkward, unfamiliar way. They sit, Jenna letting out undignified honks of sadness as Ash self-consciously comforts her with one hand, the other keeping the box of hoover waste steady on her lap.

'I didn't want – I didn't know – I feel so...' Jenna gulps down air in between words.

Then, as suddenly as they arrived, the tears stop, and Ash's hand feels even more cumbersome resting on her former girlfriend's back. Jenna places her own hand on top of the cat's makeshift Nike casket.

'Thank you for loving our baby until the end.' Her eyes bulge with sincerity as she takes Ash's hand, which stiffens at her touch. 'Let's go say goodbye.'

So, they walk, hand in sweaty hand, into the garden. There they solemnly dig a hole in the ground with the only tools Ash can find – a spatula and a pizza cutter. Jenna talks about memories of the cat, but every time Ash is touched or amused by a story, she remembers the outraged look on the pet's face earlier today as she stuffed it into its loathed travel carrier and guilt consumes her. Catching glimpses of Jenna's face, contorted with pain, makes the knot in her stomach tighten. If only Jenna had been *this* distressed when mourning the end of their relationship. Ash feels distanced not only from Jenna's grief but also from Jenna herself and her own obsessive, compulsive desire for them to reconnect.

Jenna starts telling a story about how Ash once locked herself and the cat out of the house whilst in the back garden.

'I came home to see two noses pressed against the glass,' Jenna says, smiling. 'Of course, even though you were starving and shivering, I was instructed to take a picture before

letting you back in. *Every* moment had to be captured for social media on pain of death.'

Ash scrunches up her nose but stays quiet. She's pretty sure it was Jenna instructing Ash and the animal to move so she could compose the 'perfect' shot. And she's certain it was Jenna who immediately posted the image, not her.

'I wasted hours of my life retaking photographs because a whisker was out of a place or a bit of litter was stuck to that furry arse,' Jenna continues with a roll of her eyes.

Ash, struck with a lightning bolt of indignation, remembers how Jenna would often make fun of her to friends for following the Hadids on Instagram yet always failed to mention she also watched them religiously on *Real Housewives*.

'Why are you so sad then?' She cuts Jenna off mid-sentence, loudly. 'It's just a box of ashes. You left. You decided it wasn't your cat anymore. And… well… the cat is dead. It doesn't care what you say about it now. It's too late.'

Jenna's mouth hangs open as Ash kneels down, putting the box into the hole they created. 'Look… I get that you're angry with me, Ash… but is now really the best time to do this? To talk this all out?'

Silently, Ash starts heaping dirt on top of the box.

'Come on, Ash…' Jenna's forehead knits together as she bounces nervously on the spot. 'We had some wonderful times but I…' She takes a breath and speaks more slowly, with real care. 'I felt as though I didn't exist anymore. I felt I was just for you and… I didn't know where I stopped and you began. Like my edges… they… weren't sharp anymore, you know? And I didn't think I could be me again if even a part of you was left. Do you understand, even a little, what I'm trying to say?'

Ash nods, suddenly a woman made of nothing but edges, crouched in front of a *very* fake cat grave.

'That's something I've always admired about you,' Jenna continues. 'You're so independent, right? You've always been your own person, and don't care what other people think.'

Ash drops her head, barely suppressing an exhalation of disbelief.

'I feel…' Jenna swallows as her voice starts to waver. 'I feel like I did this.' She gestures to the upturned dirt. 'In wishing for my own life, I felt I couldn't have any ties to you anymore, I couldn't have the cat. And now the thing I loved in this world as much as you is gone.'

As Jenna starts to cry again, Ash runs her hands across her own face. She feels her forehead sweat mix with dirt from the ground and the vacuum dust stuck to her fingertips.

She pushes her face deeper into her palms as a small bubble of laughter starts to rise up her body. It is not just the faux cat funeral that is ridiculous. Everything is ridiculous. She is ridiculous. Jenna is ridiculous. And her cat, with its acid-trip wide eyes, its penchant for sleeping inside laundry baskets and its ongoing feud with any balled-up pair of socks, is especially ridiculous.

Jenna, seeing Ash's shoulders shaking, assumes she is crying. She gently rests her hands on them and they stay this way for some time until Ash, composing herself, stands up and looks her ex in the eye. She considers telling her the truth, that the majority of what they've put in the ground is just dead skin cells and sandwich crumbs. This makes her face soften. Jenna smiles.

'So, are you seeing anybody?' Jenna asks. This time Ash's laugh is open and sharp as she looks up at the sky. Jenna gives her a playful nudge with her shoulder. 'Hey, give me a break. I'm trying to do the whole "being friendly" thing. Don't you want to know if I'm seeing somebody?'

Ash shakes her head, not at the question, but at where

she has wound up. If only she could post online about this *#MoggyMunchausen* debacle. Although she's sure Jenna would have something snooty to say about livestreaming a fake cat funeral.

So, instead, Ash does the only thing she can think of. She clamps her hands together and, somehow, the Lord's Prayer tumbles out her mouth. Jenna's eyes widen in surprise. But Ash powers on until, finally, Jenna follows suit, echoing her words. Together they stand, two atheists, heads bowed, saying a prayer for the soul of a cat who is halfway across town, shedding its thick black fur on another of Ash's mother's cashmere jumpers.

'Wait.' Jenna starts fiddling with her ear lobes. She holds out two dangling silver earrings, an expensive graduation gift from her parents. 'Remember how often these would get batted by those fluffy paws? They were always way more fun than any cat toy we'd buy.' She drops them grandly into the grave before Ash can think of a way to stop her.

'Amen,' Ash says flatly.

'Amen,' Jenna repeats.

When Ash picks the cat up that evening, she burrows her face into its soft black fur. She wonders if the cat will miss its high-profile status in the cut-throat, fast-paced world of Petstagram. She feels guilty she didn't cry at its fake funeral but knows eventually, one day, the cat will really die and then she will grieve, spectacularly, for the animal, with no Jenna and no fake social media friends to mourn alongside her.

The cat gently headbutts her forehead as its soft purr motors on. It reaches out a paw with playful curiosity and bats at one of the long silver earrings now dangling from Ash's ears.

The Red Dress

It's hard to know what to do the night before your father's rape trial begins. I settle on drinking. Wine, vodka, cider, that awful coffee liqueur people always regift. I even knock back the dregs of some cherry tequila. I continue drinking on my late-night flight down to London, returning to my childhood home for the first time since I was a teenager. My mother demanded the four-storey building in the divorce a decade ago and then never set foot in it again. She calls it her Mausoleum to Marital Woe.

I jump in an Uber at the airport.

'Miss Genie Slorah?' The driver leans suspiciously into the surname. Sinking into the backseat, I barely twitch my head in response. My surname always makes eyes catapult with excitement and, lately, disgust.

During the car journey, the trial is, of course, discussed on the radio. The driver's eyes scan me in the rearview mirror, looking for a reaction. At times like this, I usually flick an imaginary switch that fills my head with white noise, but today the static is glitching and words such as *vile* and *predatory* are getting through. Eventually, he turns the radio off, and an uneasy silence twists into my chest as I watch the yellow streetlights slosh into the black of the night. I close my eyes. When I open them again, there, standing alone in the dark, like a gleaming tooth in a decaying mouth, is the pristine white house. I turn my head and squint down our long driveway to see if I can make out the home of my best friend, Leona. Or former best friend, I guess. Either way, I can't see any lights on in the distance. Getting out of

the car, I will myself to re-enter this giant eight-bedroom property I'd once called home. Two beer bottles from duty free grind grimly together inside my rucksack.

As the Uber reverses, the driver rolls down his window.

'I hope the scumbag rots in jail,' he yells into the quiet of the night.

I still give him a five-star rating.

Once inside the cold, marble hallway, my father's lawyer calls.

'It's best to distance yourself from any emotions,' she instructs me. 'That way I don't have to constantly preface everything with concern that this might make you upset. Okay?' She never waits for an answer. 'We're fighting an uphill battle. The press is still pushing a load of neo-feminist, wannabe-woke nonsense and there's no denying it can influence juries. A female family member by his side tomorrow is going to really help counteract the optics of the allegations. As you know, we've never once said these women did not have sex with him, we're saying these women did not have *non*-consensual sex with him.'

I can't think of anything to say, so I go with, 'Hmmm.'

'Your father has paid for the flights to London, of course, plus two tickets to *Hamilton* with preshow dining. Security can escort you through tomorrow's protests.'

I twist my bag's strap around my finger while searching for the words.

'Is he going to be in handcuffs?' I ask eventually. The rasp of her sigh makes my cheeks prickle.

'We've been through all this, Genie. Can you just assure me you'll be there tomorrow? I have other calls to make.'

At around midnight, I brave a walk around the building

while swigging some rum I found in a kitchen cupboard. My mother, in month three of her 'quick break' to the Maldives, has sent a text, asking if I can find the Louboutin heels she'd been wearing when she 'kicked Sarah Jessica Parker in the shins' during an argument at an Emmys after-party.

The house does not feel like a home. There are no objects or spaces where memories are locked, waiting to be released. Everything is monochrome or shiny or, worse, both. Photographs of glamorous strangers on red carpets hang on the walls. There, laying empty, is the vast mantelpiece in the living room that once displayed my father's awards.

My mother sends another text.

'Don't wear your hair up tomorrow. Ears!'

Below her message, I see my latest draft text to Leona. My tone in this version is wildly inconsistent. One moment I'm sharing heart-warming memories and begging her for a brunch date; the next, accusing her of attention seeking for social media clout. I delete the draft. It would be pointless to send anything. I'll never get a reply. Not tonight, if ever.

As I walk up the grand staircase, the white noise returns, fizzing in my ears. It's trying to stop me thinking about tomorrow, what people might shout, how my father might look at me, who I might see. I travel closer and closer to what was once my bedroom. The white noise gets louder. I consider texting my father, but what would I say? I think of the phone call where he first told me about the allegations. Hearing his voice, crackling with pain, dejected and diminished, had only magnified those feelings in me.

'It's a total witch hunt, Genie.' His words had fractured and fragmented as they caught in his throat. I'd tried to sift through them, to find my parent again. 'You believe me, don't you? I know you do.'

Lately, he's sounded more measured, a little sturdier. But

bitterness still finds a way to snake through the cracks.

'It's just over-the-hill actresses angry I never cast them again and journalists with axes to grind. This is all supposed to have happened years ago. Why didn't they say anything at the time?'

He always asks that, over and over again. I never have a response, but it doesn't matter. He always answers for himself.

'Because, Genie, they're liars. That's what they are. Rotten, scheming, despicable liars who abandon you the second things get tough.'

I nudge open the door to my teenage bedroom. My eyes soften at the sight of the abundant lilac decor.

I look through my belongings. On the bedside cabinet is a family photo in a frame. I pick it up and study myself, miniature and styled by the '90s, gripping my father's hand. He's pointing at the camera with an easy, natural smile. In my free hand I clutch a cuddly toy kitten, Marie from *The Aristocats*. My father used to take me to Euro Disney once a month, marching us past the queues so I could sit at the front of rides and spend as long as I wanted interrogating the princesses about their animal friends. He'd sometimes play along, chiming in with his own questions. When Leona moved to the neighbourhood, we'd often invited her to come with us.

I grip the frame tightly.

She'd always been happy to accept his generosity back then.

I look at my stacks of old VHS tapes and the soft toys on the shelves. Under my bed, I find endless makeup palettes, well-thumbed *Sweet Valley High* novels, and all my Spice Girls dolls. Inside the bedside cabinet are several fluffy diaries containing the many inventions Leona and I

had planned to wow the world with. Coca-Cola lip gloss is probably a real thing now.

On the windowsill sit the few awards I had garnered at school – always for maths, much to my mother's horror – and, next to them, in all its plastic glory, is my replica Oscar for 'Best Daughter'.

I smile, remembering the grand presentation my father had concocted when he'd 'bestowed the esteemed accolade' upon me, lights flickering and his phone playing a fanfare sound effect. He'd bought it for me whilst away in Los Angeles for his first awards season. My mother had starved herself in preparation but returned alone, dismissing my starry-eyed enquiries about where my father was. In fact, it was a long month of no contact before he appeared in our doorway, booming about tales of executive meetings and mega-buck deals while he showered me with gifts, expertly ignoring my mother's icy looks.

I unfurl a poster in the corner of the room. It's for one of my father's old films and features a group of glossy, pouting faces. My eyes settle on one woman in particular. She looks different now. In the recent newspaper photos of her walking into court, her face is puffier, her eyes cloaked in a grey veil of exhaustion. On the poster, she's still young, luminous with airbrushed abandon. She'd signed her name – Tillie – by dotting her i's with hearts.

My father always loved parading me around his film sets, instructing the actors to fuss over me. I was shy at first, but eventually I worked out that I was part of the performance. I got better at putting on a doe-eyed masterclass, feigning interest in the glamorous strangers making my father money. Usually, the actresses would tell me how pretty I looked while he stood behind me, arms folded, jaw clicking. After

our little show of mutual appreciation ended, I'd look to my father and he would tap me affectionately under the chin. He always did that, even when I got older and had to hide my embarrassment.

'So, honey,' I recalled this Tillie actress asking ten-year-old me as her eyes remained fixed on my father. 'Do you want to be an actress when you grow up?'

'No,' he'd interjected, his hands landing heavily on my shoulders. 'That's not the life for Genie.' I tried to move but he rooted me to the spot, his hands like rigid electrical plates that could jolt me at any time.

'No,' I parroted. People always asked me that. But on this occasion, I added, 'I'm going to *make* movies. Like Dad.'

I looked up, ready to receive my nod of approval, but his face remained taut. It was Tillie who gave me what I was fishing for, flashing me her fridge-white smile.

'How sweet! Fancy bossing everyone around as well, do you?'

'That's enough.' His deep voice cut through her syrupy laugh. A shot of electricity crackled through not just my shoulders but her tensed frame as well. 'You're needed in wardrobe. Go.'

It was only once she'd left that he looked at me again with warmth.

'Come, sit in my chair. We'll get a picture for your mother.'

Later, I saw him affectionately tapping Tillie under the chin as she laughed, her hips tilted forwards and her manicured nails running through her golden hair. I don't remember what he was saying to her. I must have turned the white noise up really loud.

As I continue to trawl my bedroom, I open the wardrobe to find a plethora of bulky, pastel movie premiere dresses. In

amongst the explosion of taffeta, I find something different – a sleek dress. As I hold it up, the string-thin straps slip off the hanger and the dress drops obligingly to the ground. My body tenses. I nudge the dishevelled fabric with my foot.

The dress is short. The fabric very thin – the silk overlaid with transparent chiffon. It seems such a tacky, vulgar combination. And the dress is red. Very red.

I recall the skinny, uncertain fourteen-year-old version of myself on the night I put it on, pulling awkwardly at the low neckline, getting ready for a friend's birthday party. My father had walked into the room and anger flashed across his face.

'What do you think you look like,' he'd snapped, 'you stupid girl?'

I took a shaky step back, unsteady in new stilettos.

'Have you lost your mind?' he continued. 'Is this the type of girl my daughter is?'

My overly plucked eyebrows arched and my frosted lips jittered. I wasn't used to his temper being directed at me. At Mum, yes. At personal assistants, yes. At Colin Farrell, definitely yes. But never, ever me.

'Is this your way of telling me that you're some kind of little whore? Take it off.' He seemed enormous, his bulky torso and broad shoulders filling the doorframe. 'Can't you hear me?' he asked, his voice booming louder with each word. 'Take it off right now.'

My made-up face crumpled. I was once again a child. 'Dad, please…'

His eyes bulged. He lurched towards me, wrenching me off the ground as I tried to twist myself free. My legs kicked, and I felt the side of the dress rip. I gripped the fabric desperately, trying to cover my exposed skin.

'My daughter is not some disgusting little slut,' he hissed,

his hold on me tightening as his face fizzed with ever-growing fury.

'Dad,' I pleaded. 'You're… hurting… me.'

As suddenly as he had grabbed me, he let me go. I watched him almost double over, as if his anger, his displeasure, had taken hold of his very core. He unleashed an almighty howl that poured into every shadow of the room. Terrified, I fled down the hallway, his rage snapping at my heels.

My father never apologised, but the next day my mother informed me that he'd organised a car to take us to a boutique, where I bought a new dress so voluminous it could have doubled as a catering tent.

In the shop, my mother clacked her nails against the counter. She looked at me with a weary expression. 'Men with tempers are very generous, darling.'

It was the only thing she ever said about the matter. That and: 'I'll have the dress repaired. It's vintage DKNY, shame to waste it. You can wear it at college – if you hold onto your figure. Besides, the colour really livens up your complexion.'

I look down at the contorted folds of red fabric on my bedroom floor.

How could I have forgotten the fury and disgust with which my father had ripped my dress apart?

I start to text his lawyer, but my shaking hands make it impossible. I pick up the dress and go downstairs, grabbing a beer in the kitchen, and stepping outside to fill my lungs with cold night air. Nearby, shrouded by distance and the dark, is Leona's family home. I wonder if she is inside, still awake, consumed also by the enormity of tomorrow, by the complexity of the past.

I reread her one-word tweet from earlier: 'JUSTICE'. This time I click the link. A news article loads containing a timeline of all the allegations against my father.

I take a deep breath. I never allow myself to read anything like this. Two pages later, I have to stop, my breath wild and unfastened, like an unspooled tickertape of fluttering film.

I sit on the doorstep with my beer as I try to compose myself and process everything. For a long time, I stare out at nothing, seeing everything. A cold, sickly sensation shifts slowly through my body as I consider how miserable, tired and friendless I have become for my father – a man who knows what is waiting for naive girls in red dresses. Men who cannot – who will not – control themselves. I remember something I heard earlier on the taxi's radio: 'Slorah's defence insists that the alleged victims often attended meetings dressed in intentionally provocative attire.'

I look down at the red fabric still scrunched in my hand. I shake my head.

It's just a *dress*.

I read more of Leona's tweets.

'Excuses abusers make to discredit their victims no. 12: "Why didn't you say something at the time?" SPARE ME.'

One night, when Leona and I were in our first year of film school, we were waiting at a bus stop after a late-night study session, laughing about something or other, when a sudden movement behind me caught her eye and her face tightened. I turned to see a man leaning against a lamp-post. His mouth was hinged open as his tongue lolled. My eyes flicked down to see his hand was sliding up and down his exposed erect penis. Instinctively, I grabbed Leona and pulled her a few steps to the right. But the man manoeuvred himself so he was back in our vision, his hand still continuously in motion, his face gormless and glazed,

clearly enjoying our discomfort. Nobody spoke. I looked at the ground.

When the bus finally arrived, we boarded and sat silent and in shock on the top deck, holding each other's arms tighter and tighter.

I'd never once questioned why we'd just stood there, why we'd stayed so quiet, why we hadn't walked away – why we had been the ones who had felt ashamed.

Leona and I last spoke four months ago. She texted to say that my father propositioned her when she interned at his production company. She didn't go into detail, simply writing, 'His harassment was relentless until I told him that I'd tell you.' She ended her message by saying: 'I need to put some distance between us for a while.' At the time I had called her a liar, an opportunist, ungrateful, manipulative – you name it, I hurled it at her. But now, standing on my doorstep with a red dress still scrunched in my hand, my mind is a mesh of the flasher's unsettling smile and the bloodshot veins in my father's wild eyes. Perhaps, if you strip away my father's money, privilege and power, he wouldn't look all that different from the pathetic man lurking at that bus stop, satisfied with turning two girls sick with shock.

In the dark, I send a text to my father's lawyer and another to Leona.

Both say: 'I can't be in court tomorrow.' To Leona I add: 'I'm sorry. Please, can we meet.'

I finish my beer and wipe my mouth with the dress.

Dear Sophie

Dear Sophie,

Congratulations on the happiness.

Love,

Amy

DELETE.

Dear Sophie,

You look so in love. I love the dress, love the shoes, love the veil! I wish you a lifetime of love.

Love,

Amy

DELETE.

Dear Sophie,

How did you lose so much weight? I thought you were off coke. I have collarbone envy.

Love,

Amy

DELETE.

Dear Sophie,

Your pictures are deluding me into believing there is a Prince Charming out there for each of us.

I want what you have. More now than ever.

Love,

Amy

DELETE.

Dear Sophie,

I'm typing this from the comfort of my crumb-strewn sofa, wondering what you are up to right now. I keep checking my Instagram feed but nobody's uploaded anything for thirty minutes. Are you mid-first-dance, gazing into your new husband's eyes, underscored by a simpering Ed Sheeran track?

It does not pass me by that you are swirling around in a haze of romance while I sit on my sofa bleeding into an industrial-sized nappy.

Love,

Amy

DELETE.

Dear Sophie,

Finally, somebody posted the cake-cutting photo! The braids, the nude lipstick, the downcast eyes… this demure bride vibe is really working for you. No one would ever know you're one half of a couple who met during the 6am dregs of a Barrowlands rave.

Love,

Amy

DELETE.

Dear Sophie,

Living vicariously through you is all I have.

Colin has fallen asleep after his third beer, so I've paused the true-crime documentary about bank-robbing priests that he suggested we watch. I'm definitely not buying his insistence that he's here because 'this is happening to both of us'. He's just here so he can *say* he was here if anyone ever finds out.

Happening to both of us.

It certainly didn't feel like that when I was the one being wheeled down a hospital corridor as he waved me off with a copy of *Private Eye* in one hand and a breakfast burrito in the other. Although, how much sympathy can you demand from your ex-boyfriend as you reunite for one last hurrah in the abortion clinic? I might write in to Dear Deirdre's agony aunt column to find out. Maybe, as it's 'happening to both of us', I'll ask Colin to *also* wear a nappy before he fucks off back to his new girlfriend. He's so insistent on coming across as sincere during his attempt at bedside 'support' that he'd probably put it on. And I'd probably still stay in love with him.

I am the worst. Well, second worst. After Colin obviously.

Love,

Amy

DELETE.

Dear Sophie,

I will send this email this time.

I am going to get the congratulatory tone bang on. I will focus on the sacred, beautiful bond of marriage and *not* talk about how I cried in the recovery room thinking about how the only thing left tying me to Colin is gone.

Love,

Amy

DELETE.

Dear Sophie,

Colin looks so peaceful while sleeping. It's so pathetic. I just want to mould my body into his and pretend nothing has happened. Not his cheating. Not the break-up. Not the endless 'what should we do?' conversations. I want to go back to blissful delusion about the strength of our relationship.

Actually, now that I've been staring at him for so long, he's starting to look less peaceful and more… smug. Fuck, he really is smug, isn't he? With his stupid, smug, asleep face. I bet that whatever dream he's having right now, he's being a proper bell-end in it.

Why have you willingly chosen to spend a lifetime with an actual human man?

Good fucking luck.

Love,

Amy

DELETE.

Dear Sophie,

I have always liked your Ally. He might be a druggie but he's kind and he *adores* you. I'm guessing in his toast he told the story about how he knew you were 'the one' when you took his cat on a walk with a lead? I bet it was sickeningly adorable.

But tonight is just not the night for me to earnestly listen to heartfelt declarations of love. Tonight is the night for me to delve into the Netflix documentary that nobody's talking about. I really think these priests might pull this heist off, you know.

Help.

Love,

Amy

DELETE.

Dear Sophie,

I'm going to do it. I'm going to explain. I'm going to tell you that you are a wonderful friend, a wonderful bride and are now going to be a wonderful wife. I'm going to be better than this.

But first, I'm going to go take a tramadol. Maybe two.

Love,

Amy

DELETE.

Dear Sophie,

I am so sorry your marriage has been the stick with which I have mercilessly flogged myself this evening.

I want to be happy for you.

You have always been there for me. Who else do I know who can fashion nipple pasties out of beer mats when a wardrobe malfunction strikes when we're out clubbing? Who else would get us invited and then disinvited to a Drake afterparty? (I think Drake secretly loved your attempt to twerk a path into his private booth.) And who else would demand an autograph from the cloakroom attendant you insisted was one of the Krankies. In fact, it's impressive how often you misidentify people as short, elderly celebrities whether drunk or sober.

But I couldn't be there for you today. This unscheduled impregnation has been a real inconvenience to my body, my sanity, and my relationship with you.

I know I should have spoken to you about not attending. Sending a text was cowardly. And I should have been honest about the real reason I'm not there. I guess I wanted to spare you my 83rd tired recital of 'I know you told me Colin was bad news but…'

Well, I want to be honest with you now. Colin cheated on me. And when he got caught out, he just shrugged and trotted off to the problem-free other woman (the definition of problem-free being that she doesn't know she's the other woman). And I then, of course, was somehow fertilised by whatever sperm of his was still meandering inside me to

give our relationship the muddled, depressing ending it truly deserved.

When I look back, I see what you saw. How his every 'I love you' was painfully extracted and only offered to pacify and placate me. How he would become distant and cold whenever something was actually important to me. How his flat was basically serial-killer-level tidy.

But I also still see all the times we laughed.

Sophie, when I told him I was pregnant he *cried*. He said he was sorry for the way he had treated me. He sat with me for hours. In a horrible way, it was everything I had ever wanted. I do wonder if I agreed to the operation because I care more about making him happy than I care about making myself sad.

I'm looking forward to the slow and painful process of re-growing my backbone.

Love,

Amy

DELETE.

Dear Sophie,

I will cope with this on my own. Grief and pain have no business intruding on your wedding day. And it's important for me to become more self-sufficient anyway. You won't always be able to come around and critique my 3am online shopping panic orders. Recently, it's taken you days to reply when I send new Chris Hemsworth surfing photos. You've not attended drag queen karaoke for months.

I need to get used to not always turning to you in a crisis.

Hopefully, I've hit my crisis limit anyway. I've lost a baby, a boyfriend, what was left of my dignity and, now, I'm sort of losing you too. I'll be OK. I think. Although, you better keep contributing to our *Married At First Sight*

WhatsApp group.
Love,
Amy
DELETE.

Dear Sophie,

There's one final thing I won't tell you. I'll never tell you. The operation didn't have to be today. It could have been tomorrow, next week, last week, anytime really other than my closest friend's most important day. But I chose today. I chose to miss your wedding. I chose to be that person who could not look you in the eye and say 'congratulations'. I couldn't do it. Not when I was failing so spectacularly at the fundamental basics of life.

I chose to suck.

You know when we went to France on holiday and you ended up making out with that hideously sweaty ex-soap actor? In the morning, your voice cracked as you admitted how lonely you were and I promised that I'd comfort you after I threw up. I didn't throw up. I sat on the toilet, staring at my phone, wondering why Colin had not replied to my texts for two days. Then I came out from the bathroom and pretended I was fine. I took your hand and told you things were all going to work out just fine.

You met Ally a month later.

I'm still pretending. I'll keep pretending. And I'll get better at pretending soon. I promise.

I won't send this.

Sorry.
Love,
Amy
DELETE.

Dear Sophie,

Congratulations! I am so sad I couldn't be there. I can't wait to hear all about it when you get back from honeymoon.

Love,

Amy

There Should Only Be Greeks

'Oh my God. It's exactly like a Greek tragedy. There should only be Greeks.'
– Anya, *Buffy the Vampire Slayer*, Season 4 Episode 22

I. DEAD-EYED

I want to scorch their eyeballs and drain them of the gloss of sight. I want to chew on every sinew in their brain and clot their insides with concrete. Watch as they fail to resist their churning bodies grinding to a halt. I want to marbleise their solid backs and freeze those immovable arms that pin girls down. Let them become a monument to depravity, to entitlement, to 'boys will be boys'. As their faces turn into a whirlpool of regret, it's always the lips that are the last to stiffen and rest. They gasp 'please', 'don't' or 'help me'. Nothing they haven't heard – and ignored – from bodies underneath them before. Although… there was that one who muttered to me: 'Medusa, you frigid, snake-haired bitch.' I watched those hateful words lodge in his mouth as my gaze gleamed like an executioner's axe.

Once they are gone, locked forever at their worst, I stand up. Adjust my skirt in the mirror and stare with grey, flat eyes at my reflection. I reapply my eyeliner, glue my left eyelashes back on, go downstairs to pour myself a drink, turn on my record player and hope that maybe, next time, they will just leave me alone.

II. I'D LIKE TO REPORT A PROPHECY

Cassandra watches her eyes ruin with red and purple. Sees her own face bulge and whiten in desperation for breath. Her cries become formless as she tries to dislodge his grasp from her neck, her hands nothing but wisps of air.

She details her latest prophecy to the police officer standing in the hallway of her flat. She describes her ex's violence, aggression and belittling in a voice that walks a high wire, balance tilting with every step.

'He's going to kill me,' she says, looking at the officer with eyes as grim as headstones.

The officer scratches his neck. Tells her he wants to believe her. That he wishes she could show him proof. But when it's just one person's word against another's, his hands are tied.

'You won't do anything until you're zipping me into a body bag,' Cassandra says, as the future, cruel and all-consuming, twists through her mind.

The officer pats her on the arm. Offers a strained impression of a sympathetic smile. Suggests perhaps she could stay with a friend.

Cassandra sways gently in her doorway as she watches the officer pushing away into the night, darkness closing around him like a fist. How lucky, she thinks, that he'll only have to die once.

III. HELEN OF TROY TOWN, ROCHESTER, KENT

We marched for the beautiful white woman snatched from the streets. We shouted her name, voices exhausted, faces ablaze.

We wanted everyone to see how much we cared. How we were unsettled by the confidence in her sharp, green eyes that we recognised also existed in our own. Because women like Helen – in her French Connection turtleneck and flattering capri pants, with her sturdy-jawed boyfriend and bespectacled parents weeping on their doorstep – should not be discardable and forgettable, just another face flattened onto a missing poster.

Oh, the *other* woman was beautiful *too*, we said with furrowed foreheads. But we hadn't marched or tweeted or petitioned or strained to see ourselves in her kind, brown eyes. We didn't cry out her name. We could barely even pronounce it. So, when her body was finally found, each scream sliced from her throat, skin dampened by weeks of woodland dew, we were, frankly, *suspicious.* Who was this corpse to cloak itself in midnight and lose its way in the murky, shivering weeds?

You see, there are only so many women we have the time to mourn.

But Helen was different. Helen was not a sacrifice. Helen was the beautiful woman walking home from work who was snatched into thin air. The woman coveted by every camera. An enigma who police officers proclaimed as their life's duty to track down. *The face that launched a thousand Netflix documentaries.* We absorbed Helen into our consciousness and then, like endless slits of light across the horizon, beamed her into multiple lives and stories. Helen would never be forgotten. We would never let her truly die. One way or another, we would always bring her home.

Silent Retreat

They take my phone away. Correction. They take my phone away, *snidely*. And, if they look at its contents, I'll be kicked out of here for crimes against hippie wokeness. My average step count is 2,062, I only ever receive texts from Domino's Pizza and the last things I Googled were:

Is silent retreat a cult
Do people go crazy on silent retreat
Do you have to be silent on silent retreat
What is silent retreat

I rap my knuckles against the reception desk as the retreat staff continue to sift through my belongings, removing my laptop, four books, a notepad, pens and a six-pack of Dr Pepper. The sign next to me says, 'PLEASE KEEP NOISE TO A MINIMUM ON ARRIVAL'. I rap a little harder, the micro-rebellion thrilling me.

The manager – a tiny blonde – looks at me with an unaffected expression.

'Mr Turner, absolute silence commences in fifteen minutes.'

My eyes slide to her name tag. *Cedar*. Of course, that's her name. She pulls one final item from my case and the next sentence sling-shots out of me, devoid of dignity.

'Oh, come on, I'm not allowed HOBNOBS?'

Stepping inside my sorry little shared room, I press my palms into my temples. There are only thirteen minutes

and twenty-two seconds left of allocated noise-making. Yodel, recite Shakespeare sonnets, burp the alphabet, I have to fill the silence with something.

I start to mournfully sing *The Flintstones* theme tune.

Cedar issues instructions in a fuss-free room where the sole window overlooks the car park and a distant landscape of hills. I am now contractually silent.

'No communicating. No gesturing. No note-writing. No distractions of any kind.'

Everyone sits cross-legged, absorbing her words with placid, plain-faced compliance.

'No eye contact.'

I shift my gaze down to nipple level, tugging self-consciously at my Bart Simpson t-shirt. The others are all wearing loose, muted lounge clothes.

'No smoking. No photographs.'

Shifting on my mat, it feels like there are 77 different bones in my backside. I'm already stuck in a cycle of flinches and tics. Crick neck. Roll bad shoulder. Stretch back. Scratch ear. Clear throat. Repeat. At forty-five, sitting upright has become an endurance sport.

'No sleeping during meditations. No lateness. No harming of any living thing.'

My eyes, resting on the ridges of Cedar's sternum, flick upwards. She's so… blank. As if her pointy face is sheathed in ice.

'And no sexual contact.'

That does it. I instantly envisage shagging her, cigarette hanging from my mouth and a fly-swatter in each of my hands. Rules be damned.

'Take a moment to acknowledge the reason you are here.'

'It will be good for you to destress. Don't worry about money. It's my treat.'

'But –'

'You've really enjoyed meditating recently.'

'I –'

'Gray…'

My wife's voice flattens. The warmth cools.

'You can't carry on this way. And if you do, well… I won't be able to stay and watch.'

As I shuffle in search of comfort on my mat, a grim smirk settles on my face. Surely, a week of silence will be better than admitting to my wife that when I lock myself in the study, I'm not meditating. No. I'm alternating between drinking whisky, sending abusive emails to ex-colleagues and watching YouTube videos about World War II.

But, hey, a silent retreat, how bad could it be? I thought it would give me time to work on my debut screenplay. Every now and then, I'm overcome with indignation that I haven't won an Oscar yet, then I remember I've not written a single page of the script. This retreat could be inspiring – perhaps one of the characters could be mute?

'Congratulate yourself on being here. Acknowledge this moment. Think only of now,' Cedar instructs.

There are no clocks on the bare walls, or indeed, anywhere.

'Stay focused on the present. On every breath.'

I settle into my disgruntled lotus position as another spasm jolts my lower back. I sigh.

Surely, one hundred plus hours of silence will go by in a flash.

I flirt with myself in the bathroom mirror. A raised eyebrow. A mischievous twinkle. A wink. It's something to do.

A face to interact with.

I already miss faces. Craggy, jowly ones. Shiny, red, pimply ones. Faces with freckles, faces with smoker's lines, faces with bad, botched Botox.

Apparently, the no-eye-contact rule is to avoid a 'Vipassana Romance', where you fall head over heels for someone you've never even spoken to. I thought it sounded like a load of nonsense but last night I dreamt that Cedar and I enjoyed a silent yet sensual bath.

I can hear my roommate thumping around the bedroom. He's a heavy-set bloke, torso and arms coated in hair, who constantly emits non-regulation noises. Perhaps he's also here under marriage ultimatum duress or maybe he's genuinely loopy enough to consider this all worthwhile.

I wave at my reflection, conduct a blinking contest, make ghastly faces, pick at blocked pores, create as many chins as possible. But, when I leave the room, I will erase everything from my face and try to fade into the silence.

Right now, I look deep and hard into the mirror. The man looking back purses his lips and shakes his head at something only he can see.

Yet again, the words 'SUNRISE MEDITATION' stare at me sternly from the chalkboard. I've already lost track of what day it is. The gong thrash that awoke me at 4am reverberates in my head as I join the slow shuffle into the room. This retreat appears to be grinding us, glacially, towards either enlightenment or exhaustion.

My aching body eventually locks into place on the mat and Cedar's small feet patter past me. Before I can escape into my latest sexual fantasy, I'm interrupted by a loud sound powering from the speakers. Several bodies jump and a woman squawks in shock.

The noise happens again. And again. Despite this unpleasantness, the room quickly resumes its unspoken, collective pretence that this is all *totally* normal. More noises honk from the speakers. Eventually, it becomes clear that the noises are pre-recorded 'ohmms' and 'ahhhs' that make way for pre-recorded instructions from a shrill male voice.

'Visualise your loved one smiling in front of you,' the voice tells us. 'Sit with your loved one in this moment. Be still.'

The woman to my right instantly starts to weep. I resist the urge to roll my eyes, glancing up at Cedar and her pinched, still mouth. As the crying intensifies, so does Cedar's mulish serenity. Eventually, the woman flees the room and the resulting quiet seems to push the walls of the room even wider. I want the sounds of her sobs back. Figuring that complying with the pre-recorded voice might fill five minutes, I nod my head and rock forward, as if to propel myself into the visualisation task. I manage to conjure up my dead mother's misshapen blue sweater and a pair of plimsolls. Then she appears, shrivelling in her hospital bed, looking at me with hollowed, helpless eyes.

I abruptly move on.

My wife. Ah, of course, my wife. She should have been my first choice. She appears, wearing that black negligee of hers. Arms folded, eyes hooked wide, she taps her foot with a passive-aggressive force that makes her breasts jostle. I fear she can tell my commitment to the retreat has been minimal.

I try to envisage a different loved one. Perhaps my father? Although that's less love and more reluctant tolerance. Friends? Nope, none come to mind.

My wife's voice forces its way back into my head.

'Gray, why are you not thinking of our child?'

I dismiss her again. I worry where that path might lead.

'Open up the palms of your hands towards your loved one,' says the pre-recorded voice.

But there's no one in front of me to open my palms towards. No one safe. I let my mind ebb back into thoughts of noiseless sex with Cedar, envisaging us quietly climaxing in the other's shuddering, sweaty arms.

Then, I hear a small *meep*. I recognise the sound instantly and am appalled. Padding into my consciousness comes a static-furred, tabby kitten. Tina. Huh. I haven't seen her since I was… eight?

She looks at me with green orb-like eyes that take up two thirds of her small skull.

The voice says again to wish our loved one happiness. And I do. I wish Tina that. I fall victim to my aversion to sentimentality's pet-sized loophole. For about seventy-five seconds, I think of only Tina the kitten. I focus on her as she licks her paw then rubs it over her cheeks and wiry whiskers. I tell Tina the kitten – a forty-year-old furry memory – to be prosperous, safe and fulfilled.

Then my mind snaps off its leash. I think about Tina Turner. Then James Bond. Then my favourite action sequences. Then sport. Then football. I think about my work's five-a-side team. I remember that goal I scored from the other end of the pitch. I remember the text I sent the group chat after I was sacked. Nobody replied. Possibly because I called them all 'tosspots in polyester ties'. I wonder how they're getting on without me. Probably fine. My work, my wife – everybody is probably enjoying the quiet.

Tina lets out one final *meep*.

Back hunched on the dining room benches, I look out of the window at the grey fog obscuring the endless green hills. I'm considering doing a runner to the nearest pub but, given

my non-existent fitness levels, I'd almost certainly have a heart attack during my escape into the wilderness. I wonder if I'm indoctrinated yet. If, when the wolves descend on my exhausted, helpless body, I'll remember to scream or if I'll remain mute and telepathically wish them prosperity as they tear off chunks of my flesh.

I feel a hand on my shoulder. This, we have been informed, is the severest behaviour warning of all. *What could I possibly have done wrong now?* Yesterday, I was shoulder-tapped for spluttering during a 'flower breathing' session when a daffodil petal wedged itself in my left nostril.

A staff member's hand points to a sign on the wall.

'PLEASE CHEW MINDFULLY (20 – 40 TIMES).'

I look down at my plate of mashed potato, lentils and broccoli. In the silence, it feels as if every flawed, fucked-up thing about me is exacerbated and exposed. Even my gluttony.

I take a slow, remorseful bite and the blandness is overwhelming. I guess the more depressed our tastebuds are, the less our tongues will care to facilitate speech.

I can't remember what my voice sounds like. During my umpteenth 'meditation walk', while staring vacantly at a glistening spider's web, I half-convince myself I'm Australian or maybe Portuguese.

But – I move onto studying the dew droplets that sit like watery pimples on the branches – is the voice in my head even me? And am I actually *hearing* the voice in my head? Can thoughts make noise? Is this thought, this very thought right now, coming to me through a filter of sound? Everything suddenly feels formless and futile – like my thoughts are just a sketch on a pane of misted glass. I bat at the branches and watch the water spray onto the grass and the spiderweb shudder in the commotion.

Is my real voice annoying? Nasal? Do I always talk as much as I think? My thoughts are relentless, inconsequential, inappropriate and often just plain boring. Like my internal diatribe this morning about how porridge looks like hummus but hummus doesn't look like porridge. Not once have I caught myself contemplating politics or potential charitable endeavours, yet often I play a giant game of Tetris in my head that I always somehow lose.

Have I always been like this? My poor wife. No wonder she sent me here.

I complete my seventeenth lap of the small hedged garden then head back inside to aimlessly wander the halls.

'What would you like to discuss, Mr Turner?' Cedar's voice is frail, devoid of substance, as if it's frittering away from lack of use.

'Please,' I lean forward and give her my most winning smile. 'Call me Graham. Or Gray.'

These are the first words I have spoken in who knows how many days. They feel cumbersome, leaden – and I sound surprisingly Scottish.

'Mr Turner, this session lasts five minutes and I can only answer questions about your engagement with the retreat.'

I sit back and my plastic seat creaks. I've always been too late to the sign-up sheet to get a one-to-one session with Cedar. But, finally, here we are, sitting together in a glorified cupboard. Realising she is, for whatever reason, feigning resistance to my charm, I switch into my more natural mode. That of belligerent middle-aged man.

'Well…' I take an irritation-fuelling inhale. 'My back is aching, the food is diabolical, the meditations are mind-numbing and my roommate seems to be allergic to showering.'

Cedar, unblinking, says nothing.

'What can you do about these things? These things that "pertain to my engagement with the retreat"? You surely have a responsibility to keep guests from going insane with boredom and pain?'

She looks at me for a long time, unmoved, as ever.

'If pain is in your present, then acknowledge it. Accept it. Whether painful or pleasurable, both will pass.'

'What on earth does that mean?'

'If you reflect on my words, you'll find – '

'No. No reflecting. All I do is reflect. This is talking time right now. Talk to me.'

'Silence allows you to keep your mind on only the now.'

'But there's nothing going on in the now so I can't switch off. And I know what you're going to say – it's not about "switching off". I should be switching on. Listening to my body. To the sound of my knees cracking or whatever. But I can't. I think constantly. Relentlessly. Yesterday, I ran through the entirety of *Coming to America* line by line, just to pass the time.'

Cedar laces her thin fingers together as I drag my own large, useless hands across my face.

'Why aren't you talking?' I let out a muffled wail, my face squished into my hands. 'Say something.'

I look up to see Cedar's head tilt. Finally, an expression – a quizzical one – pulses across her face.

'Ask yourself why you are afraid of silence.'

I laugh. 'Sorry?'

'What are all your words trying to protect you from?'

I look away, noticing the laminated photos of meadows stuck onto the walls.

I think about work. About being escorted off the premises. I think about my dead mother. About my wife. About

the pregnancy. I quickly think about tiny Tina the kitten.

'I've had quite the year.' I try to smile but my face feels like a lift caught between floors. I clear my throat. 'How long do I have left?'

'Fifteen seconds.'

'No – no. I mean how many days left on the retreat?'

The alarm buzzes and her hand extends to the door.

I inhale deeply and try to do as the pre-recorded voice instructs.

'Follow your loved one. Go wherever they want to take you.'

Tina slinks behind a wheelie bin. My subconscious/spirit-guide-kitten is navigating me through actual garbage. Am I that embarrassingly literal?

On my mat, as that familiar numb feeling spreads through my arse-cheeks, I sniff up a perilously low-hanging string of snot.

In my visualisation, I move the bin to find Tina chewing at the remains of a Sainsbury's chicken sandwich. I feel bad; I should imagine some Whiskas or something for her. I root around for a better offering. When I open the bin's lid there's a smashed-up computer, a copy of my wife's latest self-help book, and piles of rotting baby teeth.

I hate my mind.

I look back down at Tina. She'd been a birthday present and slept so peacefully on my knee when I watched TV. I've not had a pet since.

I feel my grip tightening on the bin's grimy lid.

Looking up at me from the ground, she cocks her head inquisitively.

I force out a shrug.

Her green eyes blink slowly.

I shake my head.

She returns to eating her pre-packaged chicken.

I zone out during a sunset meditation. I think… nothing. No sexual deviancy, no self-hatred, no convoluted plot-twists for my screenplay, no palm-sized kittens. I am voided. Gone. It could be one minute, maybe ten, who knows? There are no clocks, no calendars, just gongs.

As I come to, I reacquaint myself with my surroundings, the faceless bodies and their various breaths, the white walls, the waning sun struggling to fleck colour across the sky. And I realise things are different. Somehow. Perhaps it's because there's a tight, squeezed sensation deep in the centre of my stomach. Perhaps it's because I'm actually acknowledging that feeling. I think it's been there a while. Or, perhaps, as irritation seeps back into my every pore, it's because there's a *pneumatic drill pulverising concrete outside*.

Yep, that's it. That's the source of the sound rattling every inch of my skull.

I look out of the window in disbelief just as a yellow JCB has the audacity to trundle past. I pull my hands to my temples. The others rock on their mats with quivering eyelids.

Cedar catches my eye. I hold her gaze in protest. I even dare to shake my head. Somehow her stretched, gaunt face tightens even further. I am mere moments away from a disapproving shoulder tap of doom and I don't care. My moment of meditative triumph has been ruined. Briefly, just briefly, I had been detached from the misery of being me.

As the gong sounds to announce the session's end, Cedar stands up. 'I would just like to remind guests,' she speaks in her whittled, whispered way, 'that a meditative state can be achieved in *any* environment.' Her eyes narrow as she looks right at me. 'And do remember this retreat was significantly discounted due to compulsory building work.'

I squirm in my latest lotus position attempt as the clatter of building work continues outside. I think about my wife clicking 'purchase' on her budget marriage-saver. Couldn't she have bought a round of golf for my father and me instead? There'd have been even less talking during that. As I allow myself a bitter inward laugh, my father's response to my sacking springs into my head.

'I'm glad your mother's not here to see you like this… All this failure.'

Unhappily, I'm plugged back into the neuroses of my mind.

My urge to complain is all-consuming. There's no sign-up sheet for one-to-ones with Cedar today but I still barge open the small cupboard door. But Cedar's not inside. Instead, one of the retreat participants, a mousy-haired woman in her twenties, is in there. She looks up at me from the floor. She has a mobile phone in one hand and an Oreo cookie in the other. She quickly stuffs both into her bra.

'Please don't tell anyone…'

I wave sternly at her chest area, indicating for her to hand over her contraband.

'There's no signal. I swear I was just looking at photos. I'm missing my family and I had a bad night. I promise. Please don't – '

I cut her off by pointing, once again, to her breasts. My eyes have become so manic and bulging they are causing me physical pain. I mimic biting on an Oreo. Fearfully, she reaches in to her bra and takes out the biscuit.

'I've already eaten half.'

I shush her again, looking pointedly to my hand and, finally, she gives me the food. For forty gloriously mindful chews, she watches me eat her snack.

Now I understand why they've been torturing us with such dry, plain food. The combination of sugar, trans-fat and more sugar fires up my body and makes me determined to dismantle Cedar and her stupid, insufferable silent regime. Why on earth have I been abiding by these pointless rules? What part of listening to a kaftan-wearing white woman chant and bang a bowl is going to save my marriage? And so, I conclude, I'm going to the pub. And I know just the people to get me there.

The silence was oppressing me but now *I* am oppressing the silence. A man on a mute mission. I head outside to see they've already started today's sunset meditation walk. The beginning is always the most exciting part of the whole enterprise – does the group plod clockwise or anti-clockwise around the shrubs? At the corner of the building, the walkers shuffle past what I'm really after: the construction workers' station. I can already make out their gruff, deep voices. I narrow my eyes and consider the approach that will ensure that, by the end of the evening, I'm stowed away in one of their car boots, on the way to the local tavern. Joining the walkers, I listen closely as the men talk and drill and talk and drill.

'When are we clocking off?' one asks. 'The sun's going.'

'Shall we call it a day? I gotta get back to put the little one to bed.'

'Never thought I'd see the day.'

'Well, it'll be you soon enough.'

'Aye, she's due any day now.'

I speed up, body-checking a meditator out of the way. Next time I circle back near the workers they'll be talking about football or Brexit or their bowel movements, surely. Something more palatable.

'He was tiny when he was born but on the scan they said he was a big baby. You never know, pal.'

'EXCUSE ME.'

They look around. I'm standing, right eye twitching, between two miserable little shrubs.

'EXCUSE ME.'

I march up to them. I've forgotten how to manage my volume. Words fog-horn out of me.

'EXCUSE ME.'

My face is pink and swollen as I splutter into their shocked faces.

'EXCUSE ME.' I say this over and over, again and again, with floundering, fish-on-a-hook eyes.

'You alright, pal?' One asks eventually.

That's what my colleagues asked me just before I smashed my laptop against the meeting room's glass wall.

'No. No, I'm not alright,' I said matter-of-factly. Far from it. I'd come home from hospital ten months earlier with nothing to do except search for a miniature coffin online. But I couldn't bring myself to explain that, so I just hurled the machine and watched as it split open then hit the floor. Its exposed innards sparked like gasps of breath.

'Ex-excuse me…' This time the words stammer out. My eyes dart to each man. One can't help but laugh as he shakes his head.

Swollen with indignance, I step forward, closer and closer, until I'm right up in his smug face. I move my index finger slowly to my lips.

'Shhhhhhh,' I hiss. My eyes never leave his. It works. He stops smiling. Nobody talks. Nobody laughs. Order – silence – is resumed.

I turn away from them and walk back to the garden, my whole body sparking and spluttering like that shattered computer on the floor.

I sit down a little too roughly on my mat.

'Visualise someone you love.' Same old, same old, blah blah, inner peace, blah.

I'm distracted by the pounding of my heartbeat, in my chest, my neck, my stomach, my feet. It's everywhere, incessantly knocking, commanding attention. I hear the sound of car engines as the workers drive away for the day. I hear the sound of steps and muffled voices outside the room.

This time, the pre-recorded voice tells us to visualise a loved one wishing us well. To imagine the loved one saying to us, be prosperous, safe and fulfilled.

I try. My wife is up first, back in her negligee. She'll just ask why I've got a bloody nose. Wait. I bring my hand up to my face. I don't have a bloody nose. That was before. When I was sacked. When I called my boss a 'cretinous arse-licker'. Pretty sure I swung for him first. Or maybe he did. Either way, only he connected.

My father appears, disappointment personified, his manhood affronted by the fact I'm 'doing that namby-pamby feelings crap'. I feel the sensation of trickling blood and, again, my hand moves to my nose. Nothing.

My ex-work colleagues appear. Hilarious. My dying mother appears. Not so hilarious. I lick my upper lip three, four times. It's dry. My dying mother offers me a tissue but she does not offer me a mantra of wellness.

I try visualising Cedar, then my flatulent roommate, then the guy at the corner shop where I buy my whisky. Nobody wants to wish me well. Not even my reflection in the bathroom mirror, with blood streaming from my nose, will wish

me well.

Then, of course, my little Tina appears. Tina. You've been good to me. You listen and don't judge. You'll wish me prosperity, safety, fulfilment, the lot.

The kitten slow-blinks with her trusting eyes and a chill etches its way across my body. The imaginary blood coating my nostrils suddenly dries.

I remember why Tina is a kitten and not a cat.

I am eight years old. My mother is healthy. But the kitten is not. It's so small. The vet says we were sold her too young, she shouldn't have been removed from her own mother, she'll need to be provided with milk all the time. We have a schedule. I sit and watch her lap from the syringe. She lies in my hand, shows me her pink, stretched stomach, her little paws reach out and grip my finger. But, one morning, I come downstairs and Tina the kitten is stiff on the kitchen floor.

Back in my stupid, self-indulgent visualisation, Tina is not yet dead. Tina is looking right at me. Her big eyes are so bright. When she was gone, they were different. Evacuated. Glassy. But, right now, they crackle with feelings and life. Tina is wishing me things. Things I don't deserve.

We wrapped her in one of my t-shirts and put her in a hole in the garden.

There's a hand on my shoulder. Cedar's. As her fingertips press into my skin, I let out a noise – something trapped between a shudder and a cry. I put my hand on top of hers to show my gratitude that someone is here for me.

'Mr Turner.' She leans down and her breath swirls in my ear. 'Please come with me.'

She walks me to the small cupboard. Inside, there's a serious-looking, large man standing in the corner. Cedar and I sit down.

'Mr Turner, you are welcome to talk from this point on.'

I don't say anything. My whole body feels in motion, like the churning of the sea. I can still picture Tina's tiny frame stretched out, her fur still so soft but her body rigid.

'We have to ask you to leave.'

I look at her vacantly.

'There have been multiple rule infringements. And now I have been informed of an altercation with the construction staff.'

I begin to process her words. I shake my head. I hold up my hands.

'Mr Turner, I don't understand what you're trying to tell me. You are welcome to talk.'

I look at her, brow furrowed.

'Mr Turner, you are allowed to speak.'

I cross my arms and continue to shake my head. I will not speak, not now, not after, finally... feeling.

'Mr Turner, this would be a lot easier if you accepted our decision and – '

I put my hands to my forehead and slouch forward into my lap. This has to be a test. This can't be it. I push myself upright and try to explain. I make a gesture to create tiny Tina and pat her imaginary body. I mime suckling at a milk bottle. I try to communicate through elaborate, wild, emphatic gestures that now is not a good time to force me to make any kind of noise, that I have just hit upon something meaningful. That silence is important. To me. Right now. Necessary. I need it.

The man in the corner and Cedar look at each other. Again, I get the dreaded shoulder tap. This time from the man.

'Mr Turner, let's go pack. Your wife is on her way to collect you.'

I look at Cedar in disbelief. Tina's wish of prosperity, fulfilment and happiness can't have been in vain. I have to try to get better. I have to fix my marriage. I have to fix myself.

I jerk my shoulder to get the man's hand off me. I try, one final time, to get them to understand. I mime the drilling, the flatulent roommate, the Dr Pepper confiscation, the sore back, the woman stuffing Oreos into her bra, the monotony, the nipple-gazing, the computer smashing, the dead kitten in my T-shirt being placed in the ground, the football matches at work, the punch up with my boss, the drinking in the study, the plot outline of my soon-to-be written Oscar-winning screenplay , the sheer volume of war documentaries I've recently watched and, then, I'm gesturing about my wife, about her pregnancy, about the scans, about the nerves and the excitement of finally becoming parents later in life, so unexpectedly, and then I'm gesturing – gesturing because there are no words to articulate the horror – about our son slipping from between her legs, still and silent. And I'm crying. Noisily, messily crying for the very first time since we lost our boy.

I sit outside the retreat, drinking a warm can of Dr Pepper. The sun sets and I try to count the shades of orange as they blend and blur into the sky. My phone, still turned off, sits by my side. It's so quiet; I can hear the sound of the leaves in the breeze and the distant clink of cutlery in the retreat's dining room. I can hear my own breath and the tick of my pulse. A pulse I have that my son does not.

My wife will be here soon. I try to think of what I will say to her. But nothing comes to my mind.

Gina

Gina, my friend who's not really my friend, tells me I have 'daddy issues'. She acts like she's making this startlingly profound insight but, really, she's just avoiding talking about cry-calling her weed dealer ex. I heard her on the phone to him through the bedroom wall the other night. Again. Gina says I only ever fall for distinguished, grey-haired men who announce on first dates that they'll never be tied down.

'We'll just have fun, Vika, sugar, OK?' She does this sleazy wink when impersonating them. I really should stop telling her so much.

But, as we sit side by side in yet another bar, sucking frothy cocktails through straws, and two guys stride over to guess where our accents are from, then call us stuck-up sluts who should smile more, and Gina tells them – with pin-prick to the artery precision – that we're not interested in their 'tiny, disease-splattered dicks', well, then suddenly she seems bearable. An acceptable accomplice for the evening. Plus, she's pretty. We take really good photos together.

'It's crazy how similar we are,' she says, as we clink our latest drinks.

'How's that?' I ask, pretending not to be offended. People constantly assume we're sisters. It's as though nobody's seen two blonde Eastern Europeans in Prada mini-skirts before.

'Oh, you know what I mean, Vika,' A disingenuous smile writhes its way across Gina's lips. 'We're just two fucked-up girls hoping that, one day, daddy might love us.' She says this oh-so-casually, wearing her pain like a silky smooth slip.

'Hmmm,' I contribute, flicking my own impression of a

smile across my face. On and off. Blink and it's gone.

Gina laughs playfully. Blows me a kiss. Nothing thrills her more than conflict and, more specifically, the likelihood of getting slapped. But I put on a show of ignoring her, sipping my drink as I look around the noisy, packed bar.

Liquid sugar ribbons its way through my insides.

Earlier in the day, my mother had visited the university flat that myself, Gina and two plump British girls share. She'd cleaned every inch of our dingy kitchen then sat in my room on the edge of my single bed. As she sipped instant coffee, her hang-dog face scanned my bare, off-white walls. Conversation with my mother remained a trudge. She looked at me blankly every time I tried to explain what a Digital Art degree was and I *definitely* didn't care about the goings on at her local Slavic Women's Institute. I'd turned down several afterparty invites to be hangover-free for her visit. So, as I endured a pill-by-pill breakdown of her backpain medication, I couldn't help but wish it had been me, not Gina, sending 5am hot-tub selfies with the Scotland rugby team reserves.

At 3pm, Gina rose from her bed to appear in my doorway, infuriatingly fresh-faced, wearing a black tasselled dressing gown.

'You must be Vika's *mummia*?' She gasped, clutching her chest like a 1920s movie star.

I snorted at her amplified accent but, of course, my mother's curiosity was piqued, allowing Gina to launch into the most sympathy-inducing excerpts from her so-called war-torn childhood. Failing to mention, of course, that she'd been on the first private jet out of there before she was two years old. I watched as my oblivious mother nodded solemnly along, the frown lines between her eyebrows digging deeper and deeper.

'But, what about *you*?' Gina asked her breathily, so good at feigning empathy and masking her dirt-digging agenda. Utterly devoted to making sure everybody – even my own mother – liked her more than they liked me. 'You must have sacrificed *so much* yourself.'

I warned my mother multiple times, in multiple languages, to keep quiet, but it was pointless. She saw it as her daily obligation to depress and be depressed. So, she began listing the horrors. Her sister's leg blasted off by a bomb. A brainwashed cousin languishing in a cell. The half-crumbled family home with bullet shell casings scattered across the decimated floor.

I flicked my finger against the bedroom blind as my mother's narrative reached the moment she'd bundled up four-year-old me and fled in the dark of the night. Then, without explanation, she stopped and walked over to my bookshelf. She plucked out the ratty copy of *1984* that I'd never told her I'd brought to university, pulling out the faded photograph I'd certainly never told her I hid within the pages.

My whole body tensed.

'This was the worst loss of all,' she said, her face spider-webbing with sadness. Gina looked down at the photograph of my handsome, youthful father holding fat, splotchy baby-me.

'He's dead?' Gina asked, her eyes flicking over to me. I stiffened further.

'Yes,' my mother replied, her voice like ash.

'But I'm confused, Vika, you told me you were estranged from your dad,' Gina said, with a scrunched-up forehead and a Barbie-doll pout. 'You said he wanted nothing to do with you.'

My mother turned to me looking for an explanation, her expression both horrified and bewildered. But, in the

immediacy of the moment, under the crush of Gina's sceptical smirk, there was no time to acknowledge my mother or her pain.

'Well, sure, we don't *know* he's dead,' I replied as caustically as possible, walking over to my mother so I could take back the book my father had owned since he was a schoolboy, his cartoon inkings still adorning the inside. I held it loosely by my side as though it was nothing to me. Like I could lose it tomorrow, like it wasn't my world.

'And sure, enemy bullet in the head is the most likely theory.' I tapped a well-manicured nail to my temple. 'But, we can't rule out the possibility that he survived the war and just ran off with some new woman to start a new life with a new family.'

My mother shook her head, mouth sloping more dramatically downwards than ever. In the long silence that followed, my brash smile faded, my father's book now a lead weight in my hand.

'Gee, lighten up,' I tried letting out an easy-going dash of laughter but it came out directionless and limp. 'Just a bit of gallows humour.' I shifted uncomfortably on the spot, trying to ignore the sting reverberating in my cheeks. 'I'm *sure* he's dead in a ditch somewhere – a hero to the resistance and all that.'

'So, tell me,' Gina said, her face flushed with delight. She twirled her dressing gown tie around her finger as though wielding a whip. 'Do you gals have fun afternoon plans?'

But now it's the evening and, tucked into the safety of a dimly-lit bar, Gina and I can pretend it's all fine, that we only want the best for each other and jealousy doesn't crouch like panthers in the irises of our eyes. My mother has hurtled back home on that long, lonely train and

my father remains a long-vanished man in photographs I sometimes kid myself I remember being taken. Tonight is for drinking and dancing – for shining in the dark – and Gina is the only person I can stand to be alone alongside, who understands I want to both dissolve and dazzle into the night. So, I allow two suited men to buy us drinks and reward them with gemstone eyes and show-pony hair flicks. I bury my embarrassment at how easily Gina had extracted the painful, most private parts of my family's past that I'd scattered deep within me like shards of shrapnel. I pose for a photo with the men, laugh about nothing so the flash catches me at my best. But, as Gina feigns interest in their anecdotes, I find myself digging inside for that last remaining secret, one final buried shell. I locate it, lodged deep in the centre of my sternum where my breath often catches and swirls. I hold my secret for a second, feel its familiar, dull ache, before pushing it deeper inside. Gina can't know everything, can't have every bit of my flesh.

As I applaud the sparkling silver bottle arriving at our table, I think of the last time I saw my father. How we stood apart, either side of the invisible line on the dusty ground that divided the saved and those needing to be saved. Only women and children could cross that day. All the men had to stay. I think of how my father reached towards me and puffed out his chest as the soldiers pushed him back, his eyes locked on the little girl screaming out for him, begging the world to let him stay with her, for terrible things to happen to somebody, anybody, else.

The magician performing card tricks for our table plucks the ten of spades from behind my ear. I can't block out the memory of my father's voice as he tells me, 'Daddy will be with you again soon, Vika; I'll find you, I promise I will.' When you discover at such a young age that even the most

wonderful people will lie to you, you'd be a fool to let yourself fall for a lie again. A home can become rubble, a man can become a ghost.

Gina stands up, bored with the men in suits now, her contractual obligation to be grateful for their generosity expired. She sashays to the dancefloor in a corseted contraption pilfered from my wardrobe. Of course, I follow her. The dancefloor is my favourite place to be. On the light-up tiles, there are no divides, nobody's lies can reach me. I can be nineteen; an empty body with a boombox for a heart and musical notes blocking out the memories. So, I hold Gina's hand and spin and whirl her like spraying champagne. People are watching our every move and their envy makes us think we are special. That the present can outrun the past. Soon the gaudy neon of a new bar will beckon. Then another. And another.

There's never enough of the night.

Later, during a lock-in at a speakeasy, we play truth or dare with the grey-haired owner, his mistress and her overly contoured friends. We learn what everybody's favourite sexual position is, and which Division Two football players have slipped into whose DMs. Then, Gina shows off her party trick of a high-heeled cartwheel into an effortless splits. I'm dared to kiss a dumpy brunette and dutifully oblige but later, in the toilets, I criticise her 'lizard tongue technique' and she overhears. Things escalate and Gina, defending my right to bitch about whoever I want, winds up smashing a bottle against the wall because why calmly illustrate your point when the option of chaos and volatility exists? As the glass shatters, it speckles everybody's skin. I don't flinch. I brush the crystal shards from my jacket and pull out a £20 note. The owner waves my hand away but I notice his eyes

crinkle. He's half-bemused, half-aroused. Typical. Out of earshot from his mistress, I agree to go to dinner with him next week.

'You look after that troublesome sister of yours, darling,' he calls out to me as we head to the door.

'Bye Vika's new daddy,' Gina coos as I drag her by the hand to the door.

Outside, we wait for our taxi and take pictures of our long-legged shadows in dewy pools of streetlight. We lament the predictably of men being charmed by unpredictable, beautiful girls.

'What's it going to take,' Gina asks nonchalantly as she checks her reflection in her phone's camera, 'for us to ever go too far?'

I pick a shard of glass out of her hair.

At 3.45am, Gina and I smoke alone on the balcony at a house party. I ignore the sickly rush from the nicotine as she starts to talk about *her* father who died when she was 14.

'When they divorced, he said I couldn't be his.' Her exquisite face seems to harden and set as if she's wearing her pore-minimising face mask. 'He took my mum to court, publicly called her every disgusting name under the sun, spent hundreds of thousands of pounds trying to erase me from his life.' She shrugs. 'Well, the DNA test proved him wrong.'

She stretches out her cigarette-holding hand until it is fully extended over the balcony railing. She waits for the burning tip of her cigarette to crumble, watching the embers float four storeys down to the ground. There's still some blood drying around her knuckles from the bottle she hurled into the wall.

'I never saw him again after that.' She purses her lips before rattling off the next sentence at gunfire pace. 'Apparently his

fourth wife was on holiday when he died. Nobody found his body for eleven days.' She pulls a face then shrugs. 'His funeral was fancy though, I saw the photos online.'

A smile slinks its way across her lips.

'Imagine, a United Nations' ambassador at your funeral – that would be cool. I'd settle for, I don't know, an internationally renowned fashion designer snorting cocaine at my wake.'

I roll my eyes like I know she wants me to. Yet, I'm still very aware she hasn't directly addressed my mother's visit, the peculiarity of my father-shaped lie. Perhaps she never will. Perhaps she likes how diminished I feel indebted to the kindness of her silence.

'A deadbeat dad always seemed easier than a dead dad,' I find myself saying, with a voice that starts firm but quickly fritters its strength away. Gina looks right at me. For once, she doesn't say a word. 'Girls with deadbeat dads get clasps on the shoulder, people pulling "sturdy" faces at them with stupid, tucked-under chins. But girls with dead dads get gawped at like insects trapped in amber. I never wanted anybody's pity. I just wanted to be...'

The words I'm too embarrassed to say out loud knock against the inside of my head: 'impenetrable', 'enviable', yes, maybe even 'dazzling'. But, as Gina waits, her eyes locked on me, I let my voice trail off into nothingness.

Gina nods, twirling her wrist as the cigarette burns closer to her sliced-and-diced fingertips. Eventually, she leans forward and narrows her eyes.

'Vika, I want you to know I never touched a single penny of my father's child support payments.' She taps her perfect teeth, as bright as a grenade's blast. 'Even when I got my veneers done.'

She sits back and I feel a swell of gratitude and admiration.

I really must be quite drunk.

But maybe it wouldn't be too bad to be like Gina. Sure, I dress better and actually read the articles in *Vogue,* but Gina is independent and fun-loving and, yes, she's nosey and competitive, but I *did* rifle through her room once and was delighted to discover medicine for a fungal toenail infection. And, *of course,* Gina is more prone to emotional, occasionally violent outbursts – at least the taxi driver she refused to pay only kidnapped us for one-and-a-half blocks – but I'm not without passion, without *feeling*. I keep my father's copy of *1984* and use his photo as my bookmark and, half an hour ago, I sat in the toilet drafting a long apology text to my mother. I thanked her for her visit, complimented her expert kitchen cleaning and asked to go with her to the Slavic Woman's Institute meeting next time I'm home.

I really need to make sure I don't go home anytime soon.

I watch as Gina furiously types a text that's definitely intended for her dodgy ex. My bare arms have started needling with the early morning cold. I pull my knees up to my chest. The chill, the alcohol, the company; I feel pleasantly anaesthetised by all of it. Like you could hurl all the glass in the world at me and I would never be hurt again. No, I can do better than that. A half-smile falls across my face. Anaesthetised like a girl who has never experienced terrible things, who's never been hurt at all. A girl with a father who is waiting up at home right now for her, pacing the living room floor.

Gina frowns at her phone, no doubt selecting an emoji to arouse or admonish her ex. I laugh to myself. Gina is OK. I hope she thinks I'm OK too.

On my way to the bathroom, I stumble past some people hunched over a frost-speckled mirror, all talking, not one

listening, about their passion for grime. I root around in the bathroom cabinets, pocketing some interesting-looking tablets that might help with tomorrow morning's sore head. I spy some Savlon cream and, returning to the balcony, throw the tube at Gina's feet.

'For the scratches on your hands,' I say.

Gina puts her phone in her bag, stretches out her body like a cat and looks for a long time at the red cuts on her right hand.

'Thank you,' she says, before dabbing on a pea-sized amount of cream. Her eyes flick up. 'Have you seen the older guy in the kitchen?' That awful, smug smile settles back on her face. 'He's just the kind of guy you like to fuck. Grey in his temples and beard. Kind of hot if he didn't have a paunch. Perfect daddy issues fodder.'

I groan and tell her to fuck off but I can't help but laugh. I throw one of my high heels at her but it misses and shoots over the balcony. She laughs as well and hurls one of her own shoes back at me, only for it to miss and end up in a plant pot. My laughter becomes louder, uncontrollable, delirious – the kind that, when I see it taking hold of others, I roll my eyes, jealous of the messy vulnerability that comes with having actual fun. I laugh – snort-laugh even – with Gina, my friend who isn't really my friend, my rival and my (sort of) rock.

I laugh and laugh and laugh until I need to throw up in a plant pot.

All the Ways We're Hurting

My living room is filled with too many family members with too many opinions, who all say 'Ellie, your son is a nightmare, you have to do something before it's too late,' so I listen with a set jaw and blank eyes as each person states their case, mentioning such times as when he flushed his uncle's prescription pills down the toilet, bit his friend's ear in drama class, stole five DVDs and a Coca-Cola, showed pornography to his cousins and, his most recent offence, hacked into my Facebook and updated my status to 'Ellie Ray is a Dirty fukin wHORE'. And they thrust its cruel glow into my face as they ask 'why on earth haven't you deleted it yet?'

My family wait, expecting my face to crumple, but I am looking at the corner of the room at the new chip in the plaster. Something akin to shame skuttles down my spine as I re-hear last night's sick thud of skull rebounding off that exact spot after my fifteen-year-old son told me he wanted nothing to do with me, that I disgusted him, that his father had told him the reason he has a new wife and son was because *I* cheated, *I* ripped the family's stitches out, so he's going to go live with his dad now and will never have to see me again. And there was such a swell in his whippet-thin frame, such vile pleasure spiking across his soft, sweet face that when he spat out the word 'slag', I saw his father standing there, lost in screams, leashes of spittle dragging across his wild, angry mouth. So, I propelled myself forwards and pushed my son, pushed him too hard, momentarily forgetting that he was not his father, not even a man, still a

half-formed boy stunted by the bitterness of a marriage that died with no dignity. As my child stumbled backwards with wide eyes and a hand stretching out for help, he connected sharply with the wall and began to whimper and flail, fists fast like a typhoon, so utterly desperate to keep me away that, as I rushed forward to hold him, he smacked into my cheek with his panicked, wild, relentless force.

I continue to stare at the chip in my wall, ignoring the intervention's expectant stares. I wonder where my son is, in what particular ways he's hurting, and think of how relieved my family will be when I confess that he's gone now, his attention-seeking antics unable to outrage them anymore. But. I don't respond to my family yet. I give my son that little bit more time; I let him find himself in the dark, sit with his rage and his broken plate of a heart, let him phone his father, let him learn how wanted he really is. I must give him this silence, this space, because, really, what else can I do?

And, finally, I start to cry.

I touch my face where he struck me, the same part of my cheek his small, rosy hand used to reach out and stroke when I rocked him to sleep. And I wish he had hit me harder. I wish he had left a bruise.

Every Shard, Every Speck, Every Particle

'I devote my energy... to self-obliteration.
However, I will not destroy myself through art.'
– Yayoi Kusama

Mai covered her bedroom walls with mirrors. The reflections reminded her she was still there, someone worth watching. From every corner, glass gleamed down like perfect smiles, bright enough to blind her to the blades gripped between their teeth. Her body had become disconnected. Parts of parts that couldn't quite move in sync. Eyes blinking. Hands reaching. A long leg stretching. Thought after thought that wouldn't settle, that didn't fit. She watched as her tongue scattered sentences, etching lies into the glass. *I'm fine, Mum. I'm fitting in well. Yeah, my conservatory tutors really seem to like me.*

But the mirrors would help, Mai soothed herself, as she hammered the last nail into the wall. The mirrors would make her whole again. A glass girl. Complete.

You're making too many sloppy errors and timing mistakes.

Mai dedicated hours to dancing in front of her mirrors. She practiced her pirouettes and pliés on pointe, perpetually in motion, constantly assessing, criticising, repeating. She was determined to get it right so everybody at the conservatory would stop telling her she was getting it wrong. From every angle, she watched her limbs extend away from

her body, each travelling higher and higher, every muscle's sinew pulled taught, as if that body part was attempting the most elegant of escapes. Mai pretended not to see her skin tremor with stress and strain. She ignored the mirrors as they echoed her pain, the glass vibrating as it stretched tighter and tighter.

You need to stop falling apart when even the slightest thing goes wrong.

The mirrors' unblinking company helped Mai scrutinise *everything*. She observed the jut of her chin, her lean legs like whittled wood, the deep grooves of her collarbone. She watched the different versions of herself multiplying down a never-ending corridor; reflecting, responding, replying to one another. Every day, all her selves brushed their hair together, read their books together, trawled their phones together, picked at their salads together. Each morning, all her selves spoke Mai's mantra, the lies ringing out like a chorus, full-voiced and strong: *You can do anything. You are capable and strong. You are the perfect dancer.*

Then, when she made yet another mistake and her body crumpled to the floor, all her selves opened their mouths and let out a scream like an axe, each trying to slash their way through the barricade of glass.

We just don't see you as the complete package.

But if her tutors really looked closely enough, they would see how much Mai wanted it, how hard she tried, how she *must* be getting it right. Mai should be the one centre-stage, not stuck behind the graceful girls always picked for the front row. Because Mai had invested everything, travelled

halfway across the world, cut off friendships and romances before they could begin, drained her parents' bank accounts, missed grandparents' funerals, nursed injuries, endured headaches, sank fingers deep into her throat, made her life nothing but mirrors. But when she tried to explain this to them, to excuse her flat feet and clumsy landings, the sentences stumbled out, her words as exhausted as her worn-out body.

In the conservatory canteen, Mai watched the other girls as they sat with full plates and laughed while making weekend plans she was never invited to.

Mai spent every evening alone. Her reflections nodded at her hungrily, encouraging her to stay.

You have been cut from the programme. Please clear your locker and leave.

When it was over, Mai had nowhere to go, no reason to leave her bedroom, nobody she dared speak to. All she could see were the mirrors and her many selves caged inside the glass. They encircled her, hunched and hollow-eyed clones, the ridges of ribcages shining through paper skin, their frail bodies trembling like leaves in the breeze.

Mai closed her eyes to find herself but, still, their reflections pierced through the dark of her lids. She had been here too long, invested too much – she'd be multiplied by mirrors forever.

One of her selves winked at her. Another rubbed her sad, tear-stained eyes. A third covered her mouth, as if stopping laughter from spilling out. A fourth walked right up to the glass and splayed both palms against it, pushing hard, willing her world to crack.

Mai tried to remember when dancing had been wonderful.

When being nine years old and doing her best was enough.

One of her selves frowned as she traced the outline of her silhouette onto the glass.

She felt the sensation of ribbons looping onto her extremities. Tugging at her. Gently, then with more force. Her body – *bodies* – her own silhouette, seemed to splinter, distend and detach, as if pulling apart and floating an impossible distance away from what she'd assumed was her core.

Her eyes blinked. Hands reached. Legs stretched. Tongue scattered. Lies, truths, mantras, apologies, everything strewn free.

She was nowhere. Everywhere. Shattered and sprayed into infinite imperfect versions. A trail of glass levitating in the air. She was this endless scattering of self, flickering with energy and emotion, contorting into astonishing shapes, leaps and spins.

Mum, she said, some part of her clutching her phone, happy to finally share a certainty, her own unbreakable truth. *I fixed it. I'm fine.*

Because every shard

every speck

every particle

was dancing.

The Scandals of Christendom

I.

Anne Boleyn called me a 'limp-haired basic bitch' last night. I'm not going to lie, it stung. I've spent most of the morning obsessively back-combing my roots.

It all started because I asked about her cruel treatment of her stepdaughter Mary. I don't know, maybe I was getting too familiar, but I suggested her behaviour *might* have contributed to Bloody Mary growing up to become a complete lunatic of a monarch. Anne said I was nit-picking. I kept pushing. She got tetchy. So, of course, she brought up what happened between me and Joely. I sighed and questioned why we couldn't talk about the manipulative, bitchy things she did for once and that maybe, just maybe, she wasn't the feminist icon the tea-towel industry wanted us to believe.

'You skim-read a few online biographies about me and suddenly you think you know it all,' Anne said as she flung my belongings across the bedroom, thumping me on the head with a well-aimed toss of my hair mousse.

'You're pathetic, Wyatt,' she hissed. 'And everybody sees it now. Everybody knows.'

Things deteriorated from there and, in the end, I went to bed crying while she sat on my bedroom floor, breathing heavily in that purposeful, attention-seeking way.

This afternoon, Anne stood imperiously behind me in the school lunch queue. When I reached the till, she leaned forward and discreetly slipped a stolen doughnut into my

hand. I was hungry and lonely, so I accepted her feeble, sugary apology and didn't mention the argument again. Instead, we skived off GCSE Spanish and went to the back of the sports hall to smoke and talk about which teacher would get the sweatiest during sex.

'Mr Daniels, obviously,' Anne said, her eyebrow inching up in anticipation of my reaction.

'Why obviously?' I asked, attempting nonchalance as she passed me the roll-up.

'Because he's perpetually damp. You of all people must have noticed.'

I shuddered but it was mainly for effect and Anne knew it. Mr Daniels always picked me to collect the textbooks from the front of class and then didn't move when I squeezed past him. He smelled like Chinese takeaway soaked in cheap aftershave and sometimes, yes, he did sprinkle sweat across my textbooks. But since Joely dropped out of school, most teachers were acting as if I didn't exist, so I appreciated Mr Daniels. He'd kept me behind on my first day back, put a hand on my shoulder and said, 'It must be really hard for you as well.' His eyes crinkled in a kind way. And he was right. It *was* really hard for me, as well.

'You want to fuck him,' Anne said, tipping ash onto the ground, looking thoroughly unimpressed.

I rolled my eyes. She was on her high horse again because she'd waited six years to sleep with Henry VIII. Or so she said.

I started hanging out with the beheaded former queen consort of England about three weeks ago. I was always going to be drawn to someone who introduced themselves as 'Anne, the scandal of Christendom'.

'I'm Wyatt, the scandal of Park Lane School for Girls,' I

replied, briefly supplanting my shame with this sharp, short thrill.

'Isn't that basically the same thing?' Anne said in a voice I chose to interpret as sincere.

We met in the school reception while I was waiting for my final mandatory counselling session. I'd been studying the Tudors for my History GCSE with Mr Daniels so I recognised her straight away. The other month, Joely and I had been paired to do a presentation on another of Henry VIII's wives, Anne of Cleves. When the two swotty girls who wore regulation-length skirts were assigned Anne Boleyn, we'd looked at each other gravely across the classroom. They'd never understand Anne's complex, ahead-of-her-time ways. But there on the tatty orange sofas outside the counsellor's office, Anne – the first Anne, the better Anne – happily chatted away to me while she flicked through a four-month-old *Hello!* magazine. And clearly Anne understood how much I understood her because, by the end of that day, she had joined my form, trained at my netball club, worked the same evening shift at the corner store, and become my new best friend.

Joely *loved* Anne.

'She was revolutionary – a woman with opinions and ambition,' she'd informed me during one of our last study sessions together at her house.

We'd been sitting cross-legged on her bed, the hip flask we were sipping from hidden at the bottom of her school bag because her mum kept poking her head around the door.

Joely continued: 'If Anne saw Kate Middleton simpering by her husband's side with her horsey hair extensions and frilly blouses, she'd glue her head back on and say it wasn't worth it.'

I nodded my head vigorously in agreement. I was always nodding my head vigorously around Joely.

And, for what it's worth, Anne quickly confirmed to me that Joely had been right. She found Kate Middleton utterly insipid – with one exception.

'She has fabulous hair,' she told me. 'So much volume.' Her eyes flicked over to me and my flattened, lifeless strands. 'Not everyone is as lucky.'

After school, Anne and I did what we always did – went to the park and sniffed nail varnish while watching people playing football. Occasionally she showed me something in the history textbook that amused or outraged her.

'Queen Anne Stuart, 1665–1714.' Her laugh shot out like a ball from a cannon. 'That family line really was cursed. Gout, obesity, and that *disaster* of a nose.'

Anne had the admirable confidence of someone who knew their charisma made their lack of beauty irrelevant. She peered closer at Anne Stuart's portrait and tutted. 'All those flattering brushstrokes and she still looks a mess. It's the 17th-century version of Chelsea Miller accidentally photoshopping out one of her boobs.'

I snorted. 'I'd forgotten about that.' Chelsea had been relentlessly mocked for weeks.

'Well,' Anne pulled a pained expression, 'the photo of Joely sort of overshadowed Chelsea, didn't it? Because in Joely's photos you could very clearly see she has two – admittedly very small – breasts. Just a shame about the whole being unconscious and half-naked thing.'

My eyes dropped to my lap.

Anne continued, clearly enjoying the glibness of her own delivery. 'If only *someone* had been there to cover her up with a nice shawl.'

'I didn't know...' My voice trailed off. I was weary of hearing my feeble defence of the infamous derailment of our last study session at my house. I didn't buy the drinks. I didn't know Joely had invited sixth-form boys. I didn't know that none of them had any intention of studying.

'Oh, I'm sure the whole thing will be forgotten soon,' Anne said matter-of-factly when she noticed I had withdrawn into myself. 'Sure, it's been 500 years and I'm still as controversial as ever, but, don't worry, I doubt you'll have the same traction.'

The sun was setting by the time we made it back home. A boy hovered by my gate. He was looking down, his sunken cheekbones and furrowed brow lit by the glow of his phone. I grabbed Anne sharply just as a wolfish smile crept across her face. The boy looked up and blushed. There were some scabbed-over spots on his chin. He looked like so many other boys: grimy but in a way you could ignore if you really wanted to.

I felt Anne yank her wrist from my grasp.

'I've... uh... I've come to study,' he said, shifting his weight awkwardly as he stared at the ground. 'Can I come in?'

My chest felt like a trap door slowly cranking open. I shook my head with wide eyes and he immediately straightened his spine, dropping the shy schoolboy act.

'Whatever, no worries. The other guys dared me to come here anyway.' He shrugged but still looked at me expectantly.

'Oh. Okay.' I didn't know what to say. I looked over my shoulder but Anne was gone. 'So, I guess you know Joely or something?'

'Not really.'

'So, you weren't… here… at the study session?' My hands twisted around the straps of my backpack. I struggled to recall the many male faces that had swum in and out of my consciousness that night.

'Nah, man, nah. I had nothing to do with all that. Like I said it's just a dare – but if you're up for something…' He took a step towards me, optimism and entitlement both dancing across his face.

'I don't…' Up close I could see these wisps of dark hair laying uselessly across his upturned top lip. But he did have nice, thick eyebrows. 'No,' I said as firmly as I could as I pushed past him. 'I don't feel like… uh… studying.' For some reason, I couldn't stop myself from adding, 'Sorry.'

Inside, I called for Anne but she didn't appear. Instead, I turned the lights on in every room, blared the television, and ate the ready meal left out for me. My mum was on night shifts again, and Anne's sudden absence felt pronounced and cruel. Like a hand tightening its grip on my throat. I flicked through my history textbook. The Stuarts bored me with their paranoid Bible antics. Henry VIII enraged me with his egotistical, sociopath tendencies. Even Elizabeth I – though I'd never tell Anne this about her own daughter – underwhelmed me. She'd lived such a lonely, distrustful life. You would have thought her mother's bold, unapologetic ways might have inspired her. Yes, it was a messy end, but I admired how Anne won and lost by doing things the way she wanted.

I reread the two pages devoted to Anne. I always found something new to mull over and made a mental note to finally ask her about the (surely untrue) allegation that she'd shagged her own brother. But the boy's smirk kept snaking through the cracks in my concentration. Perhaps I should

have let him in the house. If I was going to have a reputation, it might be more tolerable if I just embraced it.

I looked out of my window to see if there was the silhouette of anyone: a skinny teenage boy or a woman in a period gown and headdress. Either would do.

I went to the bathroom and flicked the switch. There she was: Anne, sitting on the toilet, lit up like an obscene Christmas tree topper, with her mammoth skirt hiked up so it half-obscured her face.

'Sorry, Wyatt, hun.' She gave me an unnaturally perky smile, as if the ends of her lips were pulled by strings. 'It's my time of the month. Either that or *another* miscarriage. Pass the pads.'

II.

I got a B- on my history paper and Anne's famous temper revealed itself once again.

'Oh, our argument on the reformation of the churches is a little one-sided, is it? We need to cite our sources better, do we? I *am* the source, you rank-smelling waste of space.' She stormed out of the room as Mr Daniels, who admirably never reacted to Anne's passionate displays, sat on the edge of my desk.

'Let's have a chat after school today,' he said in a low voice. 'I really think you could be an A-grade pupil, Wyatt.'

He smiled at me as I watched a bead of sweat weave through his eyebrow hairs. I didn't agree with Anne that he smelled rank. He smelled like what I imagined most men smelled like: clammy but comforting. Anything but Lynx.

However, the Mr Daniels development did not sit well with Anne.

'He should be giving me detention, not arranging a rendezvous with you,' she tutted as we debriefed behind the gym. 'The discipline issues here could really do with…' She swished her hand down with a sharp flourish, imitating her executioner's sword.

'Decapitation didn't seem to deter you from… well, anything,' I observed as I finished rolling a cigarette.

'And thank God for that. I've lived more of a life post-head-severing than anyone in this sorry little school.' She took the cigarette out of my hand before I could take a drag. 'Trust me. Being killed gives you perspective on what matters.'

'What does matter?'

'Your principles.' She looked up, her eyes slicing into me. 'I know my truth.'

For once, I wasn't sure if she had meant to barb what she'd said with passive aggressive, Joely-related judgement.

'You should try it out some time,' she added curtly. 'You know, having principles.' Ah. That was much clearer.

Mr Daniels had changed his shirt when I entered his room. His face was pink and irritated, as if he'd scrubbed it with a towel. Despite Anne's insistence that he 'wanted my nubile young flesh', I wasn't so sure. She grew up in a century when preteens were impregnated by old men riddled with syphilis. I sensed her judgement could be off.

Still, I found myself sagging into my seat when we spent the first ten minutes looking through a PowerPoint on essay writing. As he loaded a video, I looked around the room, my foot tapping against the desk's steel leg. On the wall was a tatty poster of Henry VIII, swollen with pomposity. He was surrounded by smaller headshots of the six wives. Anne, in her mini-portrait, looked indignant at being reduced to

one sixth of a support act.

I remembered something she had said to me recently while we watched a movie featuring Natalie Portman sobbing in a busty, green-sleeved gown.

'I mean… it's just ridiculous…' Anne's nostrils had flared indignantly. 'I *never* had a mole on that side of my cheek.' She sighed and inspected her cuticles. 'Dying really does get in the way of controlling your narrative.'

At that moment, my phone buzzed with a picture message. Anne watched me look at its contents, my face marbleising. I had, yet again, been sent a screengrab of the compromising picture those sixth-form boys had taken of Joely and I.

'Dying *and* mobile phones,' I added, finally prising my eyes away from my device's screen.

Natalie Portman let out a particularly melodramatic wail. Even in the dark, I could sense the roll of Anne's eyes.

In Mr Daniels' classroom, I scrutinised the poster, trying to see if there were any further misplaced moles.

Mr Daniels was still at the front, now waving his arms animatedly, endearingly excited by all the dead people who weren't Anne. I glanced at the clock in the room. Normally, I'd be in the park by now with Joely.

'Hey, what's this all about?' Mr Daniels had put his foot gently on top of mine to stop it from shaking. 'You seem distracted, Wyatt.'

I stared at his polite, brown loafer on top of my clumpy, scuffed boots. Then his foot twitched and he quickly lifted it off.

'I hear worrying things from other teachers, but I always say how engaged you are in history…'

I shrugged, still looking down at my boot, where the feel of his foot's friction remained.

'I kind of like the Tudors stuff,' I said, quickly trying to brush off the sudden awareness of my own loneliness.

'I noticed,' he said with a small smile.

'Although not the Natalie Portman film,' I added, with a very serious nod. 'It takes an alarming number of liberties with Anne's story.'

Mr Daniels couldn't stop himself from laughing.

'Right. Sure.'

'You know, I read that Anne Boleyn didn't have a sixth finger. That it was a rumour started by Catholics to prove she was a witch who cast her spell over Henry. To make it seem like he wasn't responsible for Anne's death, all the rumours, her infamy.'

This time he looked at me with a gently puzzled stare. My stomach lurched. He wasn't a Jane Seymour fan, was he?

'If you ever want to talk, Wyatt…' He started walking back to the board and I noticed little pools of sweat collecting at his armpits. 'You need to know you have people you can confide in.'

'What do you want to know?' I leaned forward, elbows on the desk, my head resting on top of my hands. Anne was often described in the history books as 'beguiling' so I widened my eyes to make myself 'beguiling' as well.

'I'd like to know how you're feeling.'

I bristled. 'I'm fine.' I resisted the impulse to glaze my face over with nothingness. 'I mean, I was upset… I am upset. What happened with Joely – it wasn't exactly what it looked like, but people have decided the photo was all my fault, so…'

'You're a sixteen-year-old girl,' Mr Daniels said. 'You're allowed to have sex.'

My cheeks prickled, but he continued to look at me calmly, as if he'd said something completely normal. Had he?

'Anyway…' He was still on the other side of the room. 'I know things are tough at the moment, especially with Joely coming back to school next week. But I – '

My burning face chilled in an instant.

'What?'

'Joely. She's back next week. They haven't told you?'

'No.' I shook my head slowly and felt plate after plate of lead drop down into my stomach. 'No, they haven't.'

Anne was sitting on our bench in the park watching *Friends* clips on her phone. A group of girls in the year below walked past and shot us a look of seething, choreographed judgement. Anne didn't acknowledge them. Nothing can faze a woman who was booed at her own wedding. I sat down stiffly beside her. On her screen a monkey clambered across David Schwimmer's shoulders.

'Henry's first wife Catherine had a pet monkey,' she said, wrinkling her nose. 'The Spanish have such basic tastes.'

'Uh-huh.' I could barely move my lips. My skin felt as if it was slowly tightening, that my mask was solidifying, leaving me rigid and blank forever. I didn't know how I could face Joely. Not now. Not yet.

Anne let out a blast of carefree laughter and I shushed her. Some boys nearby who had stopped their bikes to smoke turned to look. A tanned, stocky one with curly hair stacked into a quiff, stepped toward us. He puffed out his chest.

'I always see you here. Trying to catch our attention?'

I looked blankly back at him. Interpreting this as encouragement, he came all the way up to the bench.

'Oh, it's one of the study group girls,' he said with a snicker. 'I hear you're quite the teacher. Or is that your other slag friend?'

I could feel humiliation puncturing the numbness as I

took Anne's arm and tried to raise her from the bench.

'Come on, don't give us the good-girl act.' He licked his chapped lips as he dug into his pocket for his phone. 'We've all seen the photos. So, go on, tell us which one of the lads was the best shag?'

I stood up quickly, emitting a short, sharp yelp. I wasn't entirely sure of my next move, but the unpredictability was enough to make them back away, their cruel laughter prickling my skin.

I felt a tug backwards. Anne, now also standing, had both her hands around my left arm. She was glaring at the boys with expertly loaded loathing.

'Just leave them, Wyatt,' she whispered in my ear. 'There's bigger and better and, well, *older* things to be getting on with, don't you think?'

III.

It was odd: Anne was the one who'd given me Mr Daniels' home address, yet she spent the whole walk over there telling me I was embarrassing myself, that this was a bad idea, that I was delusional, transparent, and determined to lose my last shred of dignity and decency. I didn't say a word. I just upped my pace and listened to her barrage of disapproval. Perhaps the conjured spirit of a woman who threw a party when her husband's ex-wife died wasn't going to be my 'soul sister for life'.

Mr Daniels' house wasn't too far from mine, just a bit closer to the nicer part of town. I spotted his red car parked outside a glum-looking grey bungalow. But halfway across the road, I found myself faltering and my eyes stinging with the threat of tears.

Anne sighed aggressively. 'What is it now, Wyatt? What do you want?'

I opened my mouth, hoping the right words would fall out.

'It would be useful for you to share something because it's pretty hard to power walk in a corset.'

I made a lacklustre attempt to clear my throat. 'I want to tell him the truth,' I said eventually.

'The truth?' Anne's harsh laugh pounded the air. 'Do you honestly think he's going to understand if you tell him the truth?'

'But I didn't... I didn't mean for Joely to get hurt. I didn't even want to be with those boys. How was I supposed to stop them from taking photos of her?'

'Sure, Wyatt, sweetie. You were just a girl doing the best she could in a cutthroat world,' Anne said dryly before adding, 'and I relate to that, of course I do. But do you honestly think a sweaty, thirty-something that looks forty-something man who teaches about my "manipulative seduction" of Henry is going to relate?'

'Wyatt? What... what are you doing here?'

I froze. Mr Daniels was standing on the pavement by his house, holding a carrier bag of groceries, wearing an oversized jumper and cotton tracksuit bottoms. I tugged self-consciously at my school blazer.

'I don't, I didn't mean to... I just came from – ' I looked intensely down at the road. 'I wondered if you...'

Both Anne and Mr Daniels were looking at me with concern, apprehension, the lot. I took a deep breath and tried being someone else. A little more Joely. Or Anne. Or maybe a mix of the two. I hardened my gaze and looked directly at Mr Daniels. He took a half-step back.

'Have you seen the picture?' My voice wavered a little,

not quite conveying the steel I envisaged in my core.

He looked at me for a long time.

'I think I need to call your mum. Is she at home?'

'No, she's at work. She's always at work. Have you seen the picture?' I couldn't look away from him.

'Wyatt, it's not appropriate for you to – '

'You said sixteen-year-olds are allowed to have sex,' I spoke over him. 'I didn't actually have sex. I haven't had sex. Not properly. I just… messed around a bit. Joely did, with one of the boys. She wanted to. I think. That was before… before she passed out. But I didn't. I thought you should know that.'

Out of the corner of my eye, I saw Anne dragging her hands across her face so her skin stretched down like a bloodhound.

'Wyatt…'

'Everyone keeps saying I had sex with, like, twenty guys that night. But I didn't. Have you seen the picture? I know I'm in my bra but I have a skirt on.'

'Wyatt…'

'I didn't know they were going to take a picture. I don't really remember. There's a bottle of tequila or something between my legs.'

'Wyatt.' He spoke very slowly and firmly. 'I have not seen the picture, but I am really sorry it was ever taken and shared. For you. And for Joely.'

The cold air was starting to cut through my uniform. I wanted to step towards him and breathe in his smell, but my legs felt heavy.

'I just thought… you might have seen it.' The steel inside me had depleted. My shoulders started curling forwards.

'Wyatt…' His voice kept pushing me farther and farther away.

'Never mind.' I looked away, desperate to be somewhere else, someone else, another version of me. Without another word, I turned and started walking. For a long time, the only sound I could hear was Anne's skirt swishing beside me. For once, even she knew now wasn't the time.

'He's lying,' I finally said as I opened my front door to face spending another night in my empty, dark home. 'Everybody saw.'

I took my phone out of my pocket and opened the photo gallery. People still sent the picture to me at least three times a day, normally with an insult of choice accompanying it.

Slut. Skank. Sket. Whore. Sometimes, if they were feeling particularly cruel, they'd draw on some cartoon jizz or doodle genitalia onto our bodies. Nobody was ever particularly original. But I never deleted any of the cruel messages they sent me. I didn't feel I deserved to.

IV.

'Finally, we have somewhere to ourselves,' Joely said, pulling out not only her hip flask from her school bag, but three beer cans as well. 'And your mum isn't home from the hospital until 6am, right?'

I nodded, half-wary and half-excited for what she had planned, although I couldn't quite forget the fact that we had our history presentation the next day. Somehow Joely had managed to insert four Anne Boleyn references into our Anne of Cleves talk, and I was hoping we'd run through it one more time. I didn't want to mess up our big ending, when we'd chant 'down with the patriarchy' while Joely tore off Henry VIII's head from a picture.

But an hour later, all the alcohol was gone and Joely was

beside me on my bed, head buried in her phone. I looked up from the episode of *RuPaul's Drag Race* playing on my laptop and slid over to her. She moved her phone away from me and continued to type.

'What?' I asked with a nervous laugh.

She didn't look up, her hands still speeding across the keys.

'What?' I reached out to grab her phone but she stood up, still typing, and walked to the bedroom door.

'Some of the Year 13s from my old school are bringing round more drink and hanging with us for a bit. They're cool, you'll like them. But fluff up your hair a bit and change your top.'

Before I could answer, she was hurtling downstairs, letting out an excited shriek as she opened the front door.

We needed extra help 'studying'. That's what the text said underneath the first Snapchat picture of us with the boys. There were about half a dozen of them and we were all lounging around my bedroom. Joely was already sitting on the lap of one, his fingertips imprinting her thighs. The silver bottles of vodka they'd brought seemed luminous underneath the camera flash. I don't remember doing any studying. I remember drinking and smoking. The boys seemed older than sixth-formers, and the story as to how Joely knew them kept shifting in shape and form. The boys confused me by winking after they said things and laughing at things I said when I wasn't being funny. I remember feeling flattered when one ran his fingers through my hair as he whispered into my ear, his warm breath on my neck making my skin buzz. I remember a game involving picking cards from a deck that led to having to kiss another person. I remember Joely and I kissing after crawling to each other

on our hands and knees as the boys laughed and cheered. I remember deliberately messing up during strip poker so I could enjoy the glint of their grins while another clothing item slipped off. I remember Joely slurring, slumped on some boy's shoulder.

'We are going to get in so much trouble tomorrow when we fuck up the presentation,' she said to me at one point, a wild laugh escaping her lips.

'Who cares?' I replied, my head clouded with vodka and validation. And when Joely and one of the boys started moaning and writhing on my bed, my mouth hung open, but I emitted nothing more than a gormless, stunned noise.

The other boys told me to leave them to it, to sit back and watch. They handed me more drink. I remember that, for some reason, in the moment, it all seemed fine.

In the picture that everybody saw, Joely is sprawled across the bed. I don't know which of the boys took it. I can barely remember their faces, let alone who thought it was acceptable to take a picture of the drunk, unconscious, naked girl.

Her right leg is cocked up, tucked behind her left thigh, and her arms are splayed wide, like a discarded marionette. Her face is puckered and tilted to the side, giving her an unflattering, bulbous throat.

Everybody saw that picture. Everybody saw her yellow pants with a small, pointless blue bow, twisted halfway down her legs. Everybody saw her pert breasts and my floral duvet underneath her. Everybody saw the piles of schoolbooks stacked up on the desk behind her with the box of condoms on top. Everybody saw the many legs of the boys in the background of the photo. And everybody saw that Joely's eyes were shut. That she didn't know. That, regardless of what she might willingly have been a part of beforehand, she wasn't willingly a part of anything now.

And everybody saw me.

I'm also in the photo. At the side. You can't see much of my face, but you can see enough to tell it's me. Like my smile. You can see that. It's the broad, stiff kind, like the type they paint on clown masks at the funfair. But I'm not actually smiling. Well, technically, yes, I am. But smiling doesn't mean you're happy about something. Not always.

Everybody blames me. They say I should have stopped Joely from drinking so much. That I shouldn't have let the boys into my bedroom. That I should have told them to leave and never have allowed a situation to happen where I could be smiling while my unconscious friend had compromising, degrading pictures taken of her.

And, deep down, I agree with them. I really do.

I only really remember that there was a flash. Then laughter like knives. Next thing I knew, Joely and I were waking up in the morning to our phones blazing with judgement. The picture had been sent to everyone.

'What did you let them do?' she asked, slipping away from me in a second, her eyes locked in horror on the photo.

I delivered our Anne of Cleeves presentation a week after the deadline, looking out onto a sea of judgemental faces, while standing by myself.

v.

Mr Daniels was never going to flash me a comforting smile again. And Joely would soon be back in school, a constant reminder of my failure as a friend and as an acceptable human being.

My bed seemed the only place capable of housing my

shame. I refused to go to school. Instead, I stared at the walls, feeling as though screws were spiralling into my ribcage, restricting my breath.

Anne tried to cheer me up by playing cockfighting clips on YouTube, but eventually my non-responsiveness started to irritate her.

'It's just a picture a few snotty-nosed teens had a laugh over. God, every Catholic on the planet thinks I have six fingers and that a Boleyn familial harem – including my own *mother* – bedded my husband. You know what my motto is, Wyatt? *Never grumble.*'

I couldn't muster the energy to roll over, so I buried my face further into my pillow.

'All you do is grumble, Anne,' I countered in a muffled voice. 'You grumble about school, about tagging along with me, about your wimple giving you an itchy scalp. You were grumbling ten minutes ago about the dubstep remix of "Greensleeves" you found on SoundCloud.'

'Well, it lacked the original's timeless finesse,' Anne retorted swiftly. '*But,* I'll tell you when I *didn't* grumble – I didn't grumble five hundred years ago when I was being escorted to my execution. I didn't grumble about being killed for not producing a son. Killed so my husband could shag some bland, fertile little eye-flutterer. Instead of grumbling, I stood with perfect posture on that damn scaffolding while my executioner sharpened his sword and I praised my husband's kindness. I called him merciful and good.'

'Sorry?' I sat myself upright, startled briefly out of my misery. I looked at Anne as she inspected her nailbeds, seemingly nonplussed. 'You did what?'

'I'm pretty sure I also called him gentle. Yes, that's right. Gentle, merciful and good. And then I knelt down, said a few prayers and that blade swished straight through my neck.'

'You were using dramatic irony though, right?' I asked, leaning further forward, incredulous and appalled. 'You raised an eyebrow? You spoke with that knowing, barbed Anne Boleyn tone?'

She blinked at me slowly. She seemed genuinely confused.

'Because you know what Anne, it's actually OK that you grumble about that. You had a pretty shitty end.' My voice softened. 'You *should* grumble about him.'

'About who?' Anne asked, her spine straightening, shoulders setting back into an elegant, aligned edge.

I let out a weary laugh.

'Uh, I'm talking about your sociopath husband. Remember him? The megalomaniac with the compulsive eating disorder? The big guy with the red beard?'

Now Anne let out a short, stiff laugh of her own as she adjusted the folds of fabric on her vast skirt.

'Don't be ridiculous. He didn't know… He wouldn't have… if…' She trailed off, eyes focussed on a patch of nothing on my wall. Then, realising her lack of conviction, she pursed her lips, looked back at me and recommitted to her point. 'It *wasn't* his fault. People at court poisoned his mind, Wyatt. His advisors were frightened of the depths of his love for me. They were jealous of the control I wielded over the most powerful man in the land.' She sniffed imperiously. 'And that Jane Seymour played the unopinionated simpering flower and…'

'No, Anne.' I spoke to her with a force I had never dared speak to her with before. '*He* signed the order to kill his wife. *He* killed his daughter's mother. *He* allowed a courtroom to publicly accuse you of literally shagging hundreds of men. In three years! Do the freaking maths, Anne. That's one hell of a sex spree.'

Anne swallowed. Her eyes had become restless again,

ricocheting around my bedroom, finding nowhere to settle. Her fingers fiddled with her many rings. She was, all of a sudden, sheepish and small.

'Well,' she said, her voice as quiet as mine was now loud. 'I guess once every few hundred years or so, I do find being lambasted as some wanton, scandalous scourge a little draining.'

I nodded encouragingly, ignoring the vibrations from my phone meaning I'd probably been sent yet another abusive text message.

'And he *could* be a bit of a fat twat,' she said, in a far too solemn, small voice. I held in my desire to laugh. There was more fiddling with her rings. More shrinking of her shoulders. 'I don't know,' she added, meekly. 'It's difficult, really.'

'I understand,' I said, remembering the way those boys had made me feel. Like I was glowing and powerful, like I could shoot sparks from my fingertips. Like I had been the one in control so, surely, I must now be the one in the wrong.

'Wyatt,' Anne turned to look at me directly, her face assembled back into some form of queenly self-discipline, 'why me?'

I paused. Again, my phone angrily buzzed.

'Why not conjure up Joan of Arc or, I don't know, that indulgent ditz Marie Antoinette instead?' She was regaining her poise again, her shoulders pulled back to create her usual haughty, intimidating frame. 'Wouldn't you feel more of a kinship with say an Amy Winehouse type?'

'I just…' I felt myself slipping back into the more familiar role of awkward, inarticulate teenager. 'I guess I… sort of… kind of felt…' I wilted with embarrassment at what she was forcing me to admit. 'I felt a connection to you.' My cheeks turned candy-floss pink. 'I thought you were misunderstood.'

Unable to look directly at Anne, I sank back down onto my bed. The very bed that Joely had been unconscious and naked on. The very bed where a boy who smelled like Lynx had gently whispered in my ear. 'You tried to play the men at their own game using your brains, words, guile, and when you didn't conform, they ruined you.'

'I know,' Anne said a little stiffly, as if wary of the emotion in my voice.

I took a deep breath. 'I enjoyed the attention,' I admitted eventually, each word more uncomfortable than the last. 'I was enjoying myself. Joely asked me at one point to get her some water and I didn't. I just laughed. I laughed with them at her.'

'I know,' Anne repeated, this time a little softer.

'I was there when he was taking her top off and I did nothing. Why did I do nothing? Why did I let those boys into my house? Why did I let any of this happen?'

'Wyatt,' Anne took a deep breath. She sat down gently beside me on the bed and folded her hands neatly on top of her lap. Then, she spoke with clipped, perfect diction: 'Fuck those boys.' She paused. Took another second to compose herself. 'Fuck them all – royally. Fuck their laughter and their behaviour and their photographs that *they* chose to take and *they* chose to make public. Fuck those snickering pricks in the park. Fuck the boys who lurk outside your house hoping for a hand job and when you turn them down tell their friends you did it anyway. Fuck all the people who hold *you* responsible for being taken advantage of. Fuck Mr Daniels and his fake Mr Nice Guy act, pretending he's never once glanced down your sweater. Fuck the fucking fucks who fucked up a sixteen-year-old girl so badly they made her think the only person who'd understand her was a disgraced dead woman whose severed

body parts were dumped inside a dirty weapons trunk in an unmarked grave.'

Anne's composure was long gone. Agitated, her short, sharp breaths filled the long silence that followed. I felt my jaw shift and my eyes glisten with the grateful gloss of tears.

'Yeah, fuck them,' I said in a small, unsteady voice. Then, I added in a near-whisper. 'And fuck Henry.'

Anne paused. Her brows knitted together.

'And fuck Henry,' she eventually agreed. As much as I had needed the company, I felt bad I'd somehow brought Anne to the 21st century then mainly just smoked weed while we listened to Lana Del Rey records together. It probably wasn't much fun for Anne to sit through triple science lessons and she definitely hadn't enjoyed being in goal during a 7–0 hockey defeat. I should have afforded her death's dignity and let her continue to shape-shift through history, that legendary figure in the portrait with her wry, knowing smile. But I had tried. I'd tried to honour her complexity, to dismiss society's obsession with brandishing her as either good or bad. I'd tried to fold the pages of a history book together to create a woman, a friend, who understood how confusing, shameful and infuriating it felt to be both wrong and wronged.

'I'm sorry, Anne,' I said, my eyes locked on my bedroom floor.

Anne shrugged.

'Well, so am I,' she said, turning her head. I looked up. We were face to face again – and there was already a twinkle back in her eye. 'I'm sorry that all these years later scandals are still *so* uninspired. I mean a nude photo leak – big deal! You know, there's a whole Satanic sub-culture where people think I made a deal with the devil to have his satanic spawn.'

I wanted to be better. In so many ways. On Monday,

when Joely walked into school, I wanted to say 'sorry' to her face and accept her reaction, for better or worse. I wanted to go to the headteacher's office and hand over every cruel text message on my phone and let the senders accept the consequences, for better or worse. I wanted to walk up to Mr Daniels' classroom wall display of Henry and his Six Wives and tear it down, freeing those women from an eternity in his orbit, for better or worse.

'So,' I looked at Anne with a sad smile, unsure how much longer our time together was going to last. I chewed the inside of my mouth. Wondered how I'd like to spend the remaining moments with my one and only friend. 'Who do you think got the sweatiest during sex? Thomas Cromwell or Thomas Seymour?'

Anne pulled a face. Then she laughed, retched, and smacked my arm. Hard.

I Am a Trainwreck Actress's Vagina

I am a trainwreck actress's vagina and I just thought I'd say hello. You seemed keen to see me, the throb of your flash piercing me with its up-skirted glare. You seemed grateful when spreading me over four pages of EXCLUSIVE! NSFW! RING OF SHAME (*LITERALLY!)*! coverage in your magazines. You seemed excited when slipping words into articles like 'shameless', 'sinking', 'new' and 'low'. You kept asking 'what was she thinking!!!!???' so people would post their poorly punctuated opinions online. You all insist that, because I belong to a woman 'so vapid and talentless', I *deserve* to be exposed and degraded. Deserve to be called 'mangey, misshapen meat-curtains' by paunchy late-night TV hosts. Because you seem to believe that I – a trainwreck actress's vagina – have no right to any dignity. This *is* the mid-'00s after all. I've no right to the sanctity of fresh air underneath this VPL-free Hervé Léger dress. Instead, I deserve the throng of photographers laying down on the pavement, thrusting their cameras upwards. I deserved the online countdown to the day I became a legally penetrable orifice and I now deserve the blog-posts predicting when this body I'm part of will die. Because, what else should I expect? I am a trainwreck actress's vagina and you've reduced me to this *Basic Instinct* tribute act, legs and self-worth akimbo. You don't care that I'm bald and shivering, like one of those terrifying, hairless cats. You don't care that a musician wrote a song calling me an 'opiate-dipped flower' that 'lost its allure within the hour'. You're conditioning me to be grateful – to want the dry, pleasureless fuck of

your lens. You want me to feel flattered by the $30,000 price tag an unpixellated photo of me fetches. You don't want questioned about why the trainwreck actor's penis can rebrand as 'edgy' with a full-frontal turn in an indie with Oscar buzz. You want me to resign myself to the endless kiss-and-tells where her ex-boyfriends lie about how regularly they got me off. You want it to seem normal for me to be plucked, chafed, swabbed, insulted, cajoled, policed, scratched, rejected and never-endingly groped.

Because I am a trainwreck actress's vagina who just wanted to stay hello. I thought I'd introduce myself properly and maybe quash the rumours I'm in the throes of chronic thrush. I thought you'd like me if you got to know me. But I guess you're never going to give a fuck.

The Second Miss Thompson

When the second Miss Thompson teaches *Rebecca* to class 11C, she knows now to avoid discussing the erotic undertones. The other day she explained what 'phallic' meant and chaos engulfed the room. It started with wolf-whistling and jeers, moved onto chants of 'Perv! Perv! Perv!' and ended with one boy dry-humping and toppling the bookcase.

Instead, the second Miss Thompson talks about tension, gothic imagery, the impossibility of preserving the 'perfect' past – how rot will always find a way. In return, she's greeted with blinking, blank eyes and open mouths chewing gum, pens, and – on one occasion – a Nando's chicken leg.

She fields endless questions about Netflix's most recent *Rebecca* remake. ('How can Rebecca be fitter than Lily James?', 'Why is that lesbian maid such a straight-up bitch?' and 'For real, did that Armie Hammer dude actually try to eat someone?')

The second Miss Thompson remembers her first day as 11C's supply teacher. How she'd walked into the classroom with an optimistic smile.

'Where's Miss Thompson?' A boy, sitting with his feet on a back-row desk, asked with narrowed eyes.

'I'm here,' she replied with a pathetically hopeful wave of both hands. 'I'm Miss Thompson.'

Outrage ricocheted around the room like fireworks. It took nine minutes and two teaching assistants to get them quiet and seated again. One boy took the opportunity amidst the chaos to do a forward roll across the desks.

But, eventually, it was explained to her that she couldn't be Miss Thompson because Miss Thompson was their *real* teacher. The teacher whose tatty copy of *Rebecca* was still on the desk and whose perfume, tampons and muddy brown lipstick remained in a Chanel makeup bag in the bottom drawer. The teacher whose looped, elegant handwriting was still up there on the whiteboard. And she – whoever she was – was an intruder and a pretender who was not fit to share the Thompson name.

'I'm not gonna be taught by some lame bitch with charity-shop clothes,' one of the girls announced matter-of-factly, as if that was it, case closed.

The second Miss Thompson tried her best to pretend she wasn't intimidated by the sea of unimpressed teenage faces. She tried desperately not to let on this was her first paid teaching job.

'Well, I guess this means you'll always remember my name,' she offered that first day, with a limp half-laugh.

But every time she teaches 11c, the second Miss Thompson never feels remembered. Every lesson feels like starting again and any ground gained, any trust extracted, gets stripped away overnight, hostility to her replanted and re-enforced. It doesn't matter that she calls the essay-writing structure Point Evidence Explanation because Miss Thompson called it Point Evidence Analysis. It doesn't matter that she starts lessons with a quick quiz; Miss Thompson always started with video clips. Miss Thompson let them end ten minutes early. Miss Thompson only set homework on Tuesdays. Miss Thompson was 'better at explaining stuff'. Miss Thompson 'let me go sick bay without all these questions'. Miss Thompson 'didn't make us write so much'. Miss Thompson was 'proper buff'. Miss Thompson 'played good music'. Miss Thompson 'told us supply teachers were stupid'. Miss

Thompson 'never gave detentions'. Miss Thompson 'flirted with the dads at parents' evening'. Miss Thompson was 'a proper teacher – ain't you some kind of trainee?'. Miss Thompson 'made me actually like English'. Miss Thompson 'was so much better... Why's Miss Thompson gone all of a sudden? When's Miss Thompson coming back?'

The second Miss Thompson sends a student to exclusion for calling her an 'ugly cow' after she instructs him to remove his headphones. When he makes mooing noises while leaving, his classmates give him an exuberant round of applause. The second Miss Thompson clamps down on every muscle in her face, trying everything to avoid teetering into tears. She can't give them the satisfaction of seeing they've hurt her. She can't let them feel like they've won.

The second Miss Thompson sits in her bedroom in her cramped shared flat, planning 11c's next lesson with heavy eyes and endless open tabs. She flicks to the Facebook page belonging to her predecessor and stares at the picture of a woman with wild black curls who is laughing with abandon, her hands on the wheel of a yacht. Curling a finger absentmindedly though her own hair, she looks through Miss Thompson's copy of *Rebecca* that, for some reason, she keeps bringing home. Miss Thompson has annotated and underlined nearly every page and highlighted key quotations in thick red ink. On several pages, she's sketched a vine-leaf border just like the unkempt plants that engulfed the De Winter's decrepit Manderley home. She sniffs the pages, seeking out Miss Thompson's perfume embedded deep in the book's spine. She imagines Miss Thompson preparing for lessons with 11c. She pictures her skimming over her PowerPoints, unfazed by the challenge of teaching the most

notorious class in school. Miss Thompson would have used her experience, her personability, her calm, unflappable nature to bring them around. She envisages Miss Thompson sitting in her own, more spacious flat, tracing her finger around the rim of a whisky glass. Her well-thumbed copy of *Rebecca* on her lap, she'd turn decisively to the right page, sketching more vine leaves into the border as she mused over how best to put things, how she could enthral 11c's teenage minds. And Miss Thompson would stop, just for a second, to enjoy her favourite *Rebecca* quote, already highlighted on the page in red:

What goes on in the twisted, tortuous minds of women would baffle anyone.

Then, she'd tell the man – or maybe the woman – next to her to top up her drink. She wouldn't care that it's nearly midnight, that another school day was drawing near.

The second Miss Thompson sits on her bed, neck flushed and a small smile forming. She puts her laptop and school books away and flicks through the copy of *Rebecca*, feeling the bristle of the pages, the breeze it creates. Then, delicately, she tears out the page with the red highlighted quote.

She hopes her small act of vandalism will one day make Miss Thompson angry. She imagines her beautiful face cracking with indignity at something in her perfect life going wrong. The second Miss Thompson holds the torn page tightly to her chest. She is glad to have something – finally – that this woman does not.

The second Miss Thompson gets to 11c's classroom early. She tears down Miss Thompson's *Rebecca* wall display. She upturns Miss Thompson's messy desk drawers, watching the contents scatter across the floor: more makeup, hair mousse, unmarked papers and endless to-do notes on Post-its. She

looks through a small pink diary with 'drinks', 'catch-up' and 'birthday brunch' crammed into all the weekend blocks. Today's date is empty. Tomorrow, Miss Thompson has therapy plus a bikini and upper lip wax. The second Miss Thompson closes the diary and notices for the first time that there's a long, brown cardigan hanging in the supplies cupboard.

When the Head of English enters the classroom later, he doesn't notice that the second Miss Thompson is now wearing the cardigan. He doesn't smell the newly spritzed perfume in the air or recognise Miss Thompson's brown lip gloss is now slicked across her replacement's mouth. Instead, he offers the second Miss Thompson a longer supply contract, says they hope that she'll stay on, carry on teaching her classes, keep up her 'valiant efforts' with 11c.

His face is pale.

'I'm sorry to say that Miss Thompson has died,' he tells her in a low voice. 'It was all very sudden. We'll have an assembly tomorrow perhaps.' He pauses. Looks down at the copy of *Rebecca* on the desk. 'She always seemed… in the corridors, in the staff room, down the pub… Well, she was wonderful.'

The second Miss Thompson pulls the cardigan tighter around her and expresses her condolences, but still the Head of English stares, transfixed, at the tatty copy of *Rebecca*. Over his shoulder she can see 11c outside in the corridor, their faces peering warily in through the door's glass panels.

Eventually, she walks past her boss and opens the classroom door. 11c pour in, noisier than ever, and she gently leads the dazed head of English to the door. Without speaking, the second Miss Thompson presses play on the Hitchcock movie. The black and white iron gates of Manderley appear on screen, beauty obscured by the wilderness

that, untended, has turned the grand home into squalid disrepair. But the students are not watching, they carry on talking and laughing, lost in the urgency of being hopeful and young.

The second Miss Thompson looks down at her cardigan. She picks off a long black hair and holds it up to the light. She feels its fragile, thread-like quality between her fingers.

Then, she lets it go and watches it fall to the ground.

Anita Berber Takes Her Clothes Off Again

'We dance death, illness, pregnancy, syphilis, madness, dying, infirmity, suicide, and nobody takes us seriously. They just stare at our veil to see if they can see anything underneath. The pigs.'

– Anita Berber

The erotic dancer Anita Berber died aged 29 on December 10th 1928. Now, eighty-seven years later, I sit alone in a Berlin hotel bar, Googling the details of her passing. The cause of death is disputed. Some websites say the 'notorious' cocaine, opium, morphine and chloroform addict was found surrounded by empty syringes. Others state it was tuberculosis or toxic shock from sudden alcohol abstinence.

What they all agree on though is that, at one point in her short life, Anita Berber was the Weimer's most famous, fearless film and stage performer. Her nude dance routines and outrageous off-stage behaviour made her tabloid fodder. She left husbands for lesbian lovers, went to prison for offending the King of Yugoslavia, and once, maybe twice, stood on top of an unappreciative audience member's table and took a nice, long piss on it.

I look down at the small, marble table I am seated at – thankfully, urine free – and remind myself of the cocktail I ordered forty minutes ago. I take a sip. All around me men in suits clink glasses and couples snake hands around each

other. Everybody has a greedy look in their eyes. Nobody else is hunched over a laptop, intermittently grinding their way through work emails at 9pm.

I load another black and white image of Anita onto my screen. The smears of kohl around her eyes make them appear sunken, like they're already rotting in her skull. But her lips are doll-like, painted like a tightly ribboned bow. Below, confusing the matter further, are her exposed, ice-white breasts. She's a nightmare in a playground in a porno.

Anita died penniless and disgraced, left to the dirt in an unmarked pauper's grave. But her reputation, her legend, didn't need a headstone.

I check my texts. Nothing new, just three in quick succession from my mother.

Thea, is it cold there? BBC website says it's cold.

Dad thinks dog might be colour blind.

Upset Australia are in Eurovision Song Contest. It's just wrong.

Then, below. There it is. Received at 9.12am today. A text from 'NHS Appointment Service'.

Your biopsy result has been scheduled for Thursday.

I try to finish the rest of the cocktail in one swift, Anita-style gulp but spill some of it down my chin and onto my potentially cancer-riddled left breast. I carefully dab the fabric to avoid aggravating the swelling. An email pings through that I can't ignore from James, the online features editor. Subject line: *Do you have GOOD-LOOKING sex expert yet???!!!!!!*

The more exclamation marks James types directly equates to how sexually aroused he is by the assigned article. And he's truly frothed himself into a frenzy by dispatching me to cover Berlin Film Festival's *Fifty Shades Of Grey* world premiere – or, as James refers to it, 'that fuck-fest film with

all the spanking'. As a result, he's demanded I write several tie-in pieces while I'm here. All of them involve me interviewing German dominatrixes in sex dungeons.

I reply: *Sent sex expert copy earlier. Have also sent interview with BDSM couple and man who calls himself the 'real Christian Grey'. Watching advanced critics' screening tomorrow at 10am and will send review straight away. Premiere and after-party in evening.*

I think for a second before adding: *Did you see my pitch about the immigration documentary director? It's favourite to win the festival. Would be huge human-interest piece.*

The word *futile* burns neon-bright in my mind. I click send anyway. There's always a chance James will have a complete personality transplant that renders him able to commission articles by women about non-reproductive-organ-related issues.

A waiter appears asking if he can get me anything else.

My laptop battery is nearly dead. I didn't bring a book. 'No, nothing, thanks.'

He starts clearing my table.

'Had a good day, madam?' I snort. Because I'm thinking about James' email. Because I'm 28, alone in Berlin, and this waiter is only the fourth person I've spoken to all day. But mainly because there's probably a cancerous grenade in my breast, ready to detonate at any second.

I decide to play nice.

'Yes, it's been fine, thanks. Mainly work. Although I went on a guided walking tour this morning.'

'Ah, how lovely. Did you enjoy it?'

I look at Anita Berber's glazed, heady stare on my screen.

'We walked through the old cabaret district.'

'Very good.'

I let out a weary laugh.

'I was the only person who turned up.'

'Sounds like you got your money's worth.'

'Well...' My smile starts to strain. 'There was no hiding at the back of the pack. It was constant eye contact. Repeatedly going "mmm, how interesting" to everything the guide said.'

'And it wasn't interesting?'

'No, no, it was interesting. I learned about Anita Berber.'

'Oh.'

'You know about her?'

'I can't say I do.'

I realise I've leashed this waiter into a protracted interaction he no longer cares to be a part of.

'She was just a dancer,' I say.

'Very good, madam.' He sweeps away and the thrum of the bar fills my ears once again.

Over in the corner, a middle-aged man feeds a cherry to an escort with bulbous lips that look like lightbulbs. I go back to my room.

I arrive in the hotel lobby at 7am to start the queue for first come, first served tickets to the critics' screening. The festival's unorthodox ticket allocation protocols have no respect for my beauty sleep. But it doesn't matter because, finally, the day is here – James must be beside himself. The website's headline when I awoke was: *Fifty Shades Of Wahey! Filthy Bonk-Buster Gets Pulses Racing.*

I'm alone in the 'queue' for thirty minutes before another journalist – a tall, 40-something white guy – turns up. He makes an exaggerated show of putting headphones on so, to pass the time, I return to my phone.

I reply to an overnight text from my housemate.

No, I didn't eat your risotto. I've been in Berlin for three days.

And my mother.

Yes, I packed enough pants and socks.

Then my friend Ada.

I promise I'll smell Jamie Dornan for you and report back.

I click into the text chain with my ex. The last message I sent was during a 2am taxi journey last week.

I miss you.

No reply. I silently chastise myself for yet another display of post-break-up vulnerability.

The NHS appointment message catches my eye and the knotted worry in my chest twists tighter.

At 7.45am a new text comes through and I am far too quick, grateful even, to open it.

Wilkommen! Did you enjoy the cabaret-themed tour? Of corset you did! ;-D Feedback greatly appreciated.

I roll my eyes. The gentleman who'd hosted the tour – Hans or something suitably German – was the shiny-faced, painfully keen type. He carries a bulky laminated portfolio of stripper pictures around with him, so continued interaction is probably not the *best* idea. But, after five further minutes of queuing, with only thoughts of cancerous cell-counts for company, I text back.

Very informative, unique tour focussing on 1920s Berlin cabaret scene and the city's difficult, decadent history. Particularly insightful on lesser-known personalities, such as the iconic Anita Berber. Fascinating.

As soon as I click send, the tour guide messages back: *Danke Thea! But I meant could you post feedback on my Tripadvisor page lollll : -)))).*

It feels oddly belittling to be laughed at by a man who proudly wears a Liza Minelli t-shirt.

Super-duper you liked Anita tho. You'll LOVE this video.

I immediately click the YouTube link to find actual,

grainy footage of Anita dancing in a silent 1920s film. She mixes stuttering steps and jerking limbs with more graceful spins and stretches. Watching her in motion fascinates me anew, the way her heavily made-up face moves, how unusual her features are – a jutting chin, skull-like cheekbones and sharp, predatory teeth.

As more journalists join the queue, I shield my phone as Anita concludes her dance by wilting to the floor, arms twisted around her body like jagged thorns. Instead of finding it tragically avant-garde, I feel a disorientating thrill, like I'm in the 1920s myself, watching something ground-breaking and bold.

I realise the man behind me in thick, rectangular glasses is *Total Cinema*'s chief critic Kevin King. He's an entertainment journalism legend who interviews all the top talent – Streep, Hanks, *even* Kermit the Frog – in print and on the magazine's tie-in podcast. I silently practice introducing myself then fret about him Googling my name. I don't want Kevin King reading my 'real' *Magic Mike* strip show expose – James insisted I pose for pictures while brandishing a G-string as a lasso.

'Are you looking forward to the movie?' I clear my throat twice in amidst the seven words.

'Hmm?'

I repeat myself but, when he doesn't immediately respond, I fill the silence.

'I mean, who doesn't want to see some soft porn before lunch, right?' Not a single muscle in his face moves. 'I hope there's a goody bag. Branded bondage gear and cupcakes with iced nipples and pubic hair. That sort of thing.' I let out a desperate little laugh. 'In all honesty,' I add. 'I'm slightly dreading watching it. It looks like a faux-feminist nightmare.'

The ticket booth opens.

'I'm Thea.' I pretend the last thirty seconds haven't happened and speak in my very best, most professional journalist voice. 'I really enjoy your reviews. I'm interested in reviewing more. Just like you.' I splay my smile as wide as possible, hoping it will force him to be vaguely appreciative. 'Although not so much *this* film.'

'It's funny you should say that, Thea,' he finally speaks, giving me one of those patronising non-smiling smiles. 'I make it a rule to have zero preconceived notions about any movie I see. I'd advise anyone *serious* about covering film that they do the same.' He points to my accreditation lanyard. 'But, being vaguely familiar with your website, I'd imagine being serious is not a concern. In fact, I'm surprised the festival approved your publication access.'

He gestures towards the woman waiting expectantly for me in the ticket booth. I step away from him uncertainly. Anita Berber used to crack ungrateful audience members over the head with champagne bottles, so I turn back, the shattering of glass sounding in my head.

'It was nice to meet you,' I say in a thread-thin voice before offering a spineless smile. 'Thank you for the advice.'

Walking through the streets of Berlin on the way to the screening, I obsess over life's many woes (such as my likely cancerous demise *and* the arrogant assholery of a certain prick-faced film critic). Trying to distract myself, I recall what I can remember from yesterday's walking tour.

Berlin's onion-like layers mean that everywhere, every building, has a story. All the history, the terrible and wonderful, is squeezed and stacked into the same square-mileage, unapologetically painful and complex. I turn one corner and it's the spot where Hans told me 'here's where

half of Berlin's gay community were marched to the death camps' and, then, a few steps later he'd bust out a 'sehr amusing story' about David Bowie and Iggy Pop's cocaine escapades.

I reach a convenience shop Hans said was once a Nazi recruitment centre and, before that, a burlesque nightclub Anita and her friends frequented. Bullet marks pepper the unassuming grey marble exterior.

I go inside to buy an energy drink. As I wait to pay, I look down at the dirty, tiled floor and push down into the soles of my feet, feeling for Anita's stiletto-heeled imprints in the earth. There's a flyer on the floor for Berghain, a notoriously debauched and exclusive weekend-only techno nightclub.

The cashier laughs. 'Nicht für ein nettes mädchen.' I look at him blankly. He translates. 'Not for a nice girl.'

Before I can fake-laugh back, my phone lights up with James' number and my entire body braces.

'Thea, listen, we've had a *great* idea and you need to act fast.' He talks breathlessly, at a rate of knots, like an over-excited puppy, albeit one with a plugged nose.

'Look, the screening starts in half an hour…'

'This is important. You've got to go to a chemist or a medical shop or a hospital ASAP.'

'A hospital? Why?'

'You need to get a heart rate monitor.'

'Why?'

'So you can wear it, obviously, while watching the movie.'

I speak very slowly. 'James, why would I need to wear a heart rate monitor to watch the movie?'

'So, we can chart your heart rate to let readers know which bits will really get their pulses racing.' He lets out a mangled, giddy laugh. 'It's genius.'

'You're not serious.'

Neither of us say anything for a few seconds.

'Just sort it out. Quickly,' he finally snaps.

'You actually want to chart how turned on I am – ' The line goes dead and I'm standing, mouth hinged open, in the convenience shop. I feel caught out in my imaginary Anita footprints, like a little girl stumbling around in her mother's too-high heels.

My housemate picks this moment to message. *Your ex-boyfriend's round collecting his DVDs. You could have had the courtesy to let me know. I was exfoliating.* Then, she adds. *Btw, your share of the gas bill still needs paying.*

I consider smashing my fist against the glass door of the chilled drinks cabinet. Watch it crack and shatter onto the tiles. Anita once punched a German boxing champion square in the face and goaded him to hit her back. She wouldn't put up with a humourless housemate who writes her name onto individual eggs inside the box. Let alone a boss who drinks from a 'Top Shagger' coffee mug. I need to do something. Tip over this stand of *New! Extra-Cheesy Cheetos.* Raise absolute bloody hell in the tinned fruit aisle.

Instead, I reply to my housemate, apologising for the aftermath of my break-up inconveniencing her. I chug the entire energy drink. Already, my heart rate feels pronounced and angry, like the tumour in my left breast is giving the thump of my pulse some extra heft. I hurry to the nearest chemist and point to said breast, the same body part that was half-crushed by a mammogram three weeks ago as I listened to an efficient, sterile whirr and nerve-jamming pain shot straight through my body. Then, using Google translate, I say to the chemist: 'Ich brauche einen pulsmesser.'

The movie is not bad. Not a travesty or trashy. It's just… kind of boring. Turns out, for me, erotica isn't an ideal

match for a mass-appeal movie. The sex scenes are overly sanitised and, in my opinion, 'to butt-plug or not to butt-plug' isn't compelling enough character conflict to sustain a feature-length film. Throughout the screening, my finger is clamped into a heart rate monitor I've hidden in an empty bag of popcorn. As serious-faced critics scribe furiously whenever there's a sunlight-strewn camera shot of the female lead's back arched in ecstasy, I'm distracted by every dutiful pump of my heart. Never before have I been so aware of every precious second of my life as I waste about 7,000 of them. My mortification is sky-high; unlike my heart rate, which, after all the effort, barely fluctuates. This whole ordeal is almost as bad as when James sent me to a Justin Timberlake meet and greet dressed as Britney Spears.

Afterwards, I sit in the cinema lobby writing my two-star review and all the salacious, side-pieces James wants (such as tallying how many times bare breasts are shown). I email it across, anticipating he'll berate my lukewarm response and, even worse, my criminally steady heart rate.

But nothing. No emails or calls. It's disconcertingly quiet.

Unsure what to do with myself, I message James. *All OK?* There's two hours until the red carpet starts.

Silence.

I text my ex.

I offered to bring round your DVDs last week and you ignored me. Why today? Because you knew I was away?

He reads it instantly. No reply. No one wants to communicate with me. Not James. Not Kevin King, who avoids making eye contact as he leaves. And certainly not my ex. I was with him for three years and he won't even spare the energy to tell me to 'fuck off', that he hates me and has already moved on, no doubt busy having *Fifty Shades Of Grey* sex-fests with butt-plug-loving women.

I text Hans the tour guide.

Loved the Anita video. So provocative.

He replies immediately. I knew Hans wouldn't let me down.

Yes! To use one of your British expressions, she really didn't give two shits lol :0). If you are ever in Stuttgart, you must go see her portrait by Otto Dix.

I am – of course – intrigued.

Tell me about the Otto Dix painting, I reply.

Hans' response is the perfect distraction.

I lay in my hotel bed, already in the black H&M dress I always wear for premieres, poring over Otto Dix's *Portrait of The Dancer Anita Berber.*

Dix made no attempt to paint Anita as a beauty, that's for sure. With her head turned to the side, hand haughtily on her hip and face painted deathly white, she looks like a monstrous wonder, shockingly aged after less than three decades of decadent life.

Apparently, she was nude when posing for the image, but Dix painted her wearing a liquid red dress. The slip clings to every bone and bloat of her drug-ravaged body. The colour red drips, cries, screams, from every inch of the portrait. Her hair. Her dress. Her lips. The backdrop. All red. I can't decide what it means. Flames? Her reputation? The blood she sometimes painted onto her naked body when she danced? Infamy? Sex? Yes, *sex.* It's everywhere, engulfing her. She stands amongst it, intimately familiar yet indifferent. One hand raises the material of her dress until it rests near her crotch. See, *sex.* Slut. Provocateur. Attention seeker. As Hans described her, 'a demonic diva'. Tawdry Anita giving the headline-writers exactly what they want.

But. She's not smiling. In fact, she looks stern.

When the portrait was painted, Anita was already considered a has-been. But in the image, the woman whose style everyone once copied, whose shows they'd all come to see, whose personal troubles they'd relished dissecting, stands defiant in her decline. She knew she'd be remembered, that she'd already done enough.

There's a slithering feeling in my chest, like a python wrapping itself around yet another organ.

I ignore a call from my mother. She'll detect something is wrong no matter how many facts about Anita I bombard her with. I haven't told her about the mammogram or the biopsy. I haven't told anyone. I mean, what's there to share? Nothing's real until it's real, no matter how tightly I feel the tumour bolting into my body. Plus, well, Mum's been through this already. She has her own lightning-bolt scars. In the last five years, I've accompanied her to both her cousin and aunt's funerals.

When I look back at the image of Anita, I realise the red paint oozing all around her clearly represents death. I don't know why I didn't see it before.

Being in a red-carpet media pen is a thankless, exhausting task. You arrive long before anyone of note turns up and freeze to the bone while repeatedly being told the actors are too busy to speak. I'm hemmed in next to a cheerful Swedish radio presenter and a Dutch freelancer who elbows me in the ribs if my Dictaphone encroaches on his interviews. I secure twenty worthless seconds with the film's assistant director as he spouts inanities at me ('I'm so happy we're in Berlin') before even he's dragged away. I see Kevin King, chief film critic *extraordinaire,* actually walking the red carpet as a media guest. We're so low on celebrities the Swedish radio chap deems him worthy of an interview. Kevin proceeds to

pompously talk about the film 'revolutionising feminism on the silver screen' due to 'the prominence the application of the condom is given'. I can't help myself – an audible scoff escapes my lips. Both men turn their heads to me.

'*You* don't agree?' Kevin asks, and there's something about the way he leans so scathingly into the 'you' that, for once, I speak up.

'Not really, no. I think calling that movie "feminist" because there's one shot of a man slapping on a rubber is, forgive the pun, stretching it. Celebrating men demonstrating basic sexual hygiene, consent and decency is pretty problematic.'

They both blink at me.

'And a man championing a movie as feminist without, I presume, consulting an actual woman because the female *eventually* gets sexual gratification from the subservient role demanded of her... Well, I think that could be perceived as disingenuous and, actually, quite dangerous.'

A silence hangs in the air. Eventually, Kevin lets out a mocking puff of laughter.

'Well, you might have saved that spirited take for your own review.'

'I did,' I reply.

'Not in the article I read. The one that's been trending online for the last hour. What was the line that stood out to me? Oh, right. *The most turned on I've been since Mr Darcy took his top off.* High praise indeed.' A bewildered expression tightens its grip on my face.

'I think you're mistaken...'

'It was like a *Loose Women* confessional.'

He laughs again, louder this time, more pleased with himself. As he walks away, a cold terror crawls through my body as I load the review onto my phone.

I don't know which sentence is worse:

'He'll make more than your heart throb.'

Or

'I was turned on like a radio dial.'

Or

'Mr Grey is outrageously sexy, saucy and sumptuous, like a succulent, juicy steak.'

Or

'My cheeks were more flushed than a pair of well-whipped buttocks.'

Or

'It was all pleasure and no pain as this gal was left moaning for more.'

I try to speak, laugh, swear, but my breath has become staccato and wild.

This review, with *my* name and picture, has been posted online for the world to see and not a single clunkily manufactured metaphor is mine.

Another line reads:

'My heart rate shot into the stratosphere the first time Christian Grey flashed his droolworthy member.'

'DROOLWORTHY?!' I can't help it, the word slingshots out and my mortification reverberates around the media pen. As I grip the steel barriers in front of me, the Swedish reporter looks at me with genuine concern. 'Droolworthy…' I repeat, in a small, desperate voice, over and over again.

I want to wear something red. Unfortunately, I didn't pack anything that colour so I stay in my boring black dress for the after-party. But, when a tipsy woman leaves a red lipstick in the bathroom, I drag it across my lips. I don't suit brash tints, but that's kind of the point, it's not about

suiting, it's about *performing*. Or something. I don't know. I've had four drinks.

I toss my 'Thea' name-tag into the bin.

James wanted me to speak to the actors and ask some pointlessly demeaning questions he sent over, such as 'Would you ever do real porn?', before their publicists bundled them away. Instead, I've sent an email to James calling him *'the biggest prick I've ever met'* with a follow-up saying *'which is ironic because, according to the old receptionist, you've got the smallest prick she's ever seen'*. I've also sent a final missive saying *'I QUIT assholllllezzz'*.

I regret nothing but my spelling of assholes. Well, I also regret not knowing how I'll pay next month's rent. But, hey, I might not need to if I die soon.

I skulk around the outer edge of the party, reapplying my red lipstick then redistributing it around the rims of endless wine glasses. Everyone seems to know everyone else. They slap backs, grin sloppily and churn canapes around their mouths. They're happy to be here. Loud. Present. Alive.

I have six missed calls from James. Two from my mother. Hans hasn't replied to my last text asking what Anita's pet monkey was called. Maybe I shouldn't expect my one-time tour guide to respond to 10.48pm texts. The stars of *Fifty Shades* are cordoned behind three levels of VIP red-tape. Eventually, I manage to penetrate the first area by shimmying through some plant pots when a bouncer isn't looking, but all I get for the thorny scratches is a conversation with a German first-time director looking for a distributor for his werewolf apocalypse film. He has bruschetta crumbs stuck in his beard. For a while, we use one another to be less alone while our roving eyes try to locate more exciting conversations.

A woman with a peroxide pixie-cut compliments me on

my lipstick and I, in turn, admire the lime-green rubber catsuit she's spilling out of. She's a performance artist called Ditsy (no surname) who reached the semi-finals on *Germany's Got Talent* playing a plethora of musical instruments strapped to various body parts. Ditsy says she found the movie 'so-so', adding forlornly: 'I would have liked more nipple play.' She introduces me to her friends whose faces sparkle with piercings.

'So, what's your deal red lipstick girl?' Ditsy asks.

'I'm a writer.' The unsaid twists like a hook in the pit of my stomach. I force my smile wider in the hope I'll appear more convincing. 'My name's Anita.'

'What sort of thing do you write, Anita?' An ice-cold thrill curls through my body at her acceptance of my borrowed name.

'Oh, serious think piece articles for the broadsheets,' I say, bluffing with a lifted chin. I sink yet another drink.

She leans in closer so I can hear her over the music. She has terrible skin, coated in a thick paste of foundation.

'And what are you writing about now?'

I focus on the beat of my heart underneath the lumpy weight in my left breast. I pick up another drink from a passing waiter's tray.

'Death,' I say, grandiosely, emboldened by my identity scam. 'About how it sometimes takes facing the end to make the middle matter.'

'Death is life,' Ditsy says with a painfully sincere nod. Her dilated pupils are inky lagoons. 'It's *everything*.'

'Totally,' I reply. Alcohol will clearly not be enough to sustain me through the conversations on offer this evening. Luckily, Ditsy's friend, a part-time DJ called Kyle, sprinkles my drink with a dust he promises will 'make the good times *freaky* good'. He has a purple-tipped goatee and a Hello

Kitty tattoo on his neck. The animal's flat eyes seem to follow me no matter where I'm standing.

My insides prickle with the early embers of euphoria. I want to reach out and press my palms against the walls, push firmly and watch as the room – the evening – pulls apart into an infinite expanse.

'You know, Anita,' Ditsy says, as we stand outside in the smoking area. I'm stroking my right arm with my left hand, enjoying the delicate shudder of each tiny brushed hair. 'When you told me you are writing about death… it makes me want to share a secret.' I tilt my head to further take her in. She has huge, thick, fake, bejewelled eyelashes like raindrops resting on talons. 'I often dream about my own death.' She takes a long inhale of her cigarette. 'Sometimes two, three nights in a row.' Another flourished inhale and suspenseful pause. 'It's a vivid dream where I'm suckered down through a sinkhole.'

'Fucking hell.' I frown at her and she frowns back.

'No, Anita, not "fucking hell", think about it…' She clamps both of her cold hands around one of mine. 'It's an amazing sensation, this burning freefall. Wouldn't it be how you would want to go? Getting to see inside the crust of the earth in the seconds before it ended. Every night, I know *all* the secrets the ground beneath us holds.'

My bra is rubbing on the spot where my lump is. The ketamine's electrical currents haven't made their way there yet. I should track down Hello Kitty Kyle.

'So, what about you?' She asks. 'How would you want to die?'

I lock eyes with Ditsy and am overwhelmed, momentarily, by a desire to tell her, after less than an hour of acquaintance, that, well, this is it for me, I've fucked up, I've already

been swallowed by the sinkhole and nobody's pulling me out. I want to tell Ditsy everything, but then, across the smoking area, I notice Kevin King in a semi-circle of white, balding men. He looks over and I feel his snicker crawl across my body.

'Anita?' Ditsy nudges me. 'Do you think about your own death when writing?'

My body hums the answer, 'Yes, constantly, every miserable second, yes'. For a moment, I conflate my own demise with Anita Berber's and envisage myself dead on the floor, a decayed relic to decadence, surrounded by the empty vials of my many, many vices.

'Oh... you know,' I try and lock whatever the actual truth is somewhere safe, tuck it underneath my bra strap, alongside my swollen skin. 'I reckon I'll go out nice, clean and simple.' I whistle a falling cartoon sound-effect. 'Anvil. On my head. Like Wile E Coyote.'

'What?' Ditsy's laugh is bright and beautiful like a chandelier.

'Meep meep,' I say, imagining my body is a cartoon pancake on the floor, my tumour just an animation I could paint over or pluck out. I make the noise again, and join in with Ditsy's laughter. Her friends laugh along and the atoms and alcohol inside me laugh too, and I remember things are fine tonight, Kevin King is pointless and his presumptions don't define me, and if I make the most of tonight then my last offensively average twenty-eight years might not matter that much.

'Let's dance,' I say, wrenching Ditsy's hand back towards the entrance of the club. As we walk past Kevin King, his eyes follow me, and he goes to speak.

'Kevin,' I say, holding my hand up to him as I keep walking, 'I don't fucking care.'

Dancing is a magician's cloak, underneath which Thea slips away and Anita truly arrives. Sprinkled in the mirror-ball's light, she uses my body to shimmer and bend, vibrantly, violently, to the music. Every part of me feels like a red-lipped smirk. The ketamine digs its claws in, operating my muscles and levering my mind. It makes me dangerous and more direct. It frees me from the burden of caring what people think.

'Come on, Anita,' Ditsy breathes in my ear. 'Let me show you my city.'

And, so, I am propelled across Berlin one dancefloor at a time. From bar to club to club to bar, again and again. It feels increasingly important, essential even, to keep moving, to shake any feeling of disease or dread from my core. I do this by dancing, by reckless, unrelenting travel through light-up dancefloors, podiums, bar tops and poles.

At some point, we're driven out to Berghain and I'm walked past the long line of people queueing. Somebody we're with must be on the guest list. As the bouncer eyes me up, I remember how most people are infamously turned away at Berghain's door. I start slipping back into meekness, readying myself for rejection. But then, the drugs haul a look of entitlement back onto my face. Anita used to slap the faces of doormen who dared keep her waiting.

My hand twitches with impatience.

He waves me inside.

I walk into the most exclusive, debauched nightclub in the world, and, right on cue, one of Ditsy's friends peels the overlay off my dress so I'm just in my black slip, arse-cheeks barely covered. A sticker is placed over the lens of my smart phone and I'm pulled into a room where hundreds of glistening bodies are crammed, thumping and throbbing to the pump of techno music. The collective mass undulates to the beat as if they are the stereo speakers, like a boombox

is inside each of their hearts.

James would be beside himself that I'm here, I think, as I watch a podium dancer bend over so a member of the crowd can bite his backside. A first-person article about tonight would hospitalise him.

Very quickly, I lose sight of Ditsy and everyone I came with. I'm unconcerned. Dancing alone allows me to plunge deeper into the sinkhole of the night. I dance with the jagged twisted limbs I'd watched in Anita's video, then I switch it up, floating my body more delicately, my arms spiralling high above me like uncaged birds ascending into the sky. I keep smashing into other people but there's no need for apologies. Strangers' fingertips dig into my hipbones, some slide sweaty arms over my shoulder, German voices shout into my ears. I bite my lip at them, nod, laugh.

Away from the dancefloor, I wind through the dark corners of this huge multi-level building. I trace my hand along the sticky wall before settling down on a sofa to watch activities unfolding in dimly-lit corners. Bodies slowly grind and lips mash. The timid half-tease of *Fifty Shades Of Grey* seems another lifetime ago. I sip my drink and act unfazed.

Eventually, a woman sitting on the other end of the sofa peels away from kissing her partner and starts to delicately caress my neck. I let it happen because, this is fine, I can be mortified by work unnecessarily sexualising me and can also be some random couple's stupefied sex toy. I am my own complicated person. Hey, Anita was apparently once a sex slave for a married woman but she was also a published poet and Marlene Dietrich's muse. It's OK, I tell myself, as the woman bites my neck, to be a little bit messy.

Her partner starts to fondle my breasts, and I push myself into her touch, enjoying being wanted, unlike my ex, who looked me in the eye and said, bluntly, plainly, deci-

sively, 'no'. I like being somebody people say yes to, somebody Berghain bouncers say yes to, so I too will say yes to everything this place offers up.

I feel my bra straps slip off my shoulders and a hand hook inside one cup to release my right breast. My eyes roll back. Both women are touching, kissing, pressing into my warm, flushed flesh. I wrap a leg around one while giving the other a sly, encouraging smile. But, when my left breast is freed, the skin seems to disintegrate like ash in her hand.

I retract with a yelp, my breath lodging in my throat.

I look down at my chest.

The breast is deformed, its lilac veins engorged and tight, the skin bulging out like a watery, ballooned blister. I blink and now it looks bloody, as if smeared in the red paint of Anita's portrait. When I look again, it's covered in bandages, just like my poor mother's post-surgery chest.

The two women, heavy-eyed and soft-lipped, wait for me to come back to them. I hold my finger up, not quite able to steady my breath, and ask for one more second.

But now the breast looks rotten. Festering.

'No,' I say to the women with a ragged voice. 'No, danke.'

I'm outside the club in nothing but my slip, my breasts still exposed. I look up to see a sliver of peach cutting through the grey sky. It's morning.

My hands tentatively touch my skin. The offending area seems fine. No scabs, blood or blisters. I can't even feel the hard lump that I've prodded and pushed so many times. I notice I'm emitting a low, pathetic whine.

I want to scour myself clean. To yank my insides out. Rid myself of whatever it is that's making me stumble around Berlin in desperate search of answers, an identity, a good fucking time.

Time.

I want to have more of it. To fix the disastrous, dull choices I've been making all my life. I don't want to sit behind a desk and write bilge. I want to tell stories about interesting people like Anita or the immigration documentary-makers or the guy on my road who makes life-size papier mâché replicas of the Queen Mother. The sublime *and* the ridiculous.

I drop down onto the edge of the pavement, take my phone out of my bag and peel off the sticker.

I can see that I sent a text to my ex six hours ago, at 12.52am. I groan.

I have cancer!1!!

And there's more.

Probably.

Well, definitely. Knowing me. Finally completed the trilogy – shit job, shit love life, shit breasts.

And then finally.

If I do have cancer, spare me the pleasure of your company on my death bed.

A stranger – a woman – sits on the pavement next to me.

'Girl, are you OK?'

I can only shrug.

'You know you've got your titties out, right?' Judging from the accent, she's Australian. I nod and wipe away a tear forming in my right eye.

'Sorry,' I add.

'Nothing to be sorry for… I just wondered… can I help? I have some Molly. Would Molly help?'

I shake my head.

'Good, cause I really need to start rationing my supplies.' I can't tell if she's trying to make me laugh or if she's just being, well, Australian. 'Do you want to talk or something? I'm a pretty good listener. My mates talk a load of self-

involved shit and I sit through it all.'

I look up. The stranger is a red-haired woman wearing a black hoodie, leather trousers and snakeskin boots. Her eyes are brown, almost orange. The colours swirl into one another like stirred honey. For a while I say nothing, just appreciate her presence.

'Do you have a friend I can get?' She asks eventually, looking around at the near empty entrance.

'No,' I say, switching out of my trance, feeling the cold air once again. 'I'm alone.' I shift around to look at her. I try being honest. 'Which really sucks.'

'Oh.' Her eyes widen. She nods. 'I get that.'

'I was in a relationship for three years… and now I'm not.'

'Shit.'

'Yeah.'

'When did it bite the dust?'

My grip tightens around my phone. 'Like, two weeks ago.'

'Well, that's an absolute shitter.'

'Yeah.' I breathe out. I look down at my half-naked body on the pavement of a Berlin street. 'It really is.'

She takes off her hoodie. 'Here, put this on. Your nips look icey.'

'He just… left.' I pull the hoodie over my head and, as I do, I feel the cancer, the sadness, the something, rise up through my chest, then my throat, then crack in two and travel up each side of my face until it reaches my eyes and starts to come out as messy, loud, purged tears. I slump forward, head in my hands, elbows on my knees. 'There was no fighting. No cheating… that I know of. He just didn't love me anymore. So. He left. It seemed so easy. I just… bored the love out of him.'

The Australian woman pats my hand.

'Somehow, I really don't think *you* are the boring one.'

I snort. I think about Anita dining in restaurants wearing nothing but a fur coat and a necklace filled with cocaine. I think about her dipping rose petals in chloroform for a mid-morning treat. How a nude dancer in anything-goes Weimar Berlin still managed to amaze and appal. The Nazis tried to strip her name from the history books but she clawed her way back in. Then, I think about me, right now, splotchy-faced on the pavement. I can't even handle one night in Berlin without a half-nude meltdown.

'Do you know how it feels to be so… so spare, so insignificant that nothing you do means anything? My boyfriend walks away without looking back. My work, my writing means nothing. My friends cancel on me while I'm on the train to meet them. Even my dog prefers my dad. Like, he's my dog, my *childhood* dog and he likes my dad more.' I let out an unhappy little laugh despite myself. 'And my mum…' I think of her drained, pale face when she told me what she'd have to lose to gain more time. 'My mum deserves better. A daughter she can be proud of. Who makes a difference. Who knows how to have fun.'

I look around. Two men with matching mohawks walk past us, hand in hand. They smile sympathetically but a few steps later I hear them laugh.

My phone pings.

'Shit, it's my ex.' With panicked eyes and a tentative hand, I go to open the message.

'Do you really want to read that?' The Australian woman grabs my wrist. 'Because you just said you want to have fun.'

'What do you mean?'

She cocks her head. Her eyes crackle with some kind of electricity and there's a mischievous smile inching across

her face. I find myself smiling back.

'Do you want to have fun?' She asks, emphasising every word.

I notice that I'm nodding. Quite vigorously.

'You know…' I twist the strings of the hoodie around my finger as I push everything out of my mind that isn't right now. Like biopsy appointments. Like disapproving texts from ex-boyfriends. Like an annoying housemate I sent a voice note where I'm singing the Taylor Swift song 'Bad Blood'. 'You kind of look like this German dancer I've been reading about.'

It's 10am. My flight back home leaves in five hours. I haven't been to bed, my jaw is locked and I'm standing in the middle of a Berlin street with half a dozen Australian backpackers, some twenty-year-old break-dancer twins in latex and a beautiful Croatian woman called Sonya who's already booked a budget flight to London to stay with me next week.

Behind us, on a giant billboard, looms a poster for *Fifty Shades Of Grey* featuring only the male actor, his back turned, looking out of his glass office to a bleak horizon.

I've promised everybody that this tour will be worth it. That Hans really knows his shit.

'Thea,' he says, nervously. 'You came back so soon? And with friends.' The break-dancer twins both high-five him good morning. Several of the Australians are halfway through a tone-deaf rendition of *Cabaret*.

'Tell them, Hans,' I say, clutching his arm. 'Tell them about Anita.'

Underrated Uma Thurman Movies

'Your sister's dating her new yoga teacher.' Jay's mother rooted around in her fridge for food he hadn't asked for. 'He's that Uma Thurman's cousin.'

Jay gazed out the kitchen window, a helpless look embedded in his eyes.

'He's got a cameo in *Pulp Fiction* standing behind a milkshake counter.'

She emerged, triumphantly holding a pack of ham and three half-empty mustard jars.

'He's very tall. Like that Uma is, I guess.'

Jay flashed her a tight, obliging smile as she spread the items out on her plastic tablecloth.

'Now, I shouldn't really have told you that.' Her eyebrows shot up as she gave him her most serious of looks. 'It's early days. Cherie's not met the family yet or nothing. She has met his dog though. Says it's a bit yappy but dead cute. A Dijon fritz.'

'That's not a dog, mum, that's two different kinds of food.' For something to do, Jay spread the mustard – Dijon, actually – onto a sweaty slice of ham.

'Well, I don't know!' She held her hands in the air and sat down opposite him. For a second, it could have been forty-odd years ago, with Jay, a little boy again, sitting with his mother in the kitchen – the decor, her pastel blouse, the fake pearl earrings, the bursts of performative indignation – but then his eyes settled on her tired, frail face. 'It's some fancy-sounding breed with fur like Nana's hair, God rest her soul. Here, you ever see that dog of yours anymore, the

one you had with Katie?'

He picked at the ham's edge.

'No, she's Katie's dog now. I've told you that before.'

'Aw, shame.' She adjusted her cardigan as she wrinkled her nose.

'Penelope,' he added.

'Who?'

'Penelope was my dog. With Katie.'

'Oh yeah. Penelope. Wasn't she a sweet thing? Bit smelly. But still.' She let out a pointless but melodious little hum. 'Cherie didn't say what his dog's called.'

She looked expectantly at his sandwich. He gave in. Took a bite.

'So, what's his name?' Jay asked, mouth half-full of grease.

'Cherie didn't say.'

'No, *his* name.' He laughed in exasperation. 'Mr Uma Thurman's cousin. The very tall, yoga-teaching, milkshake-counter guy in *Pulp Fiction*. The latest wonderful man in my wonderful sister's wonderful life.'

'Oh…' She looked off into space and frowned. 'I don't remember. It was a funny one though. Probably Finnish cause she's Finnish, int she? That Uma Thurman? She looks Finnish.'

'I've no idea.' Jay scraped some mustard from his lip.

'I watched her movies after Cherie told me. Thought I should, you know. Make an effort. Took ages to download them all.'

'And?'

Her mouth sloped to the left as she struggled to be tactful.

'Bit daft aren't they. All that chopping and slicing. Not for me.'

He laughed again and, this time, she tilted her head and enjoyed the lightness skipping across his face.

'What about *The Truth About Cats and Dogs*?' Jay asked her quickly to avoid any chance of her slipping into sentimentality.

'What's that?' Her eyes widened. 'Secret cats and whosits?'

'It's an Uma Thurman movie.'

'Oh…' She looked worried. 'I didn't see that one.'

'It's underrated,' he said. 'And – good news – zero slicing to worry about.'

She fiddled with her sleeves, guilt bubbling up.

'I told Cherie I liked the movies,' she admitted in a small voice. 'I hope he doesn't ask me too much about them. You know, if I get to meet him. Cherie's a busy girl.'

'Well,' he grimaced. 'I told Cherie I liked her last fella, and the fella before that and the fella before that. In fact, last time I saw her I even pretended I was interested in her crystals or her chakras or whatever yoga-hippy-dippy fad she was banging on about.'

'She's good she is. With her health.' His mother always pretended she couldn't hear the snip in her children's voices. 'Good at keeping slim, eating well, doing all that bendy stuff. She said they're going to a garden centre this weekend.' She looked at him sternly. 'But I didn't tell you that.'

Jay had started a staring contest with a cartoon cow on his mother's biscuit jar.

'You seeing anyone, Jay? You on that Tinder looking at them silly selfie pictures?'

She scanned him up and down, mouth crinkling smaller. Jay sat up straighter, sucked his stomach in.

'All those girls with big lips like they've stuck a hoover on them?'

He rubbed at a mark on his jeans he'd somehow missed earlier.

'Cherie showed me once… Girls giving themselves animal

ears and whiskers and shiny, sparkly skin. Cherie's photos were nice though. Natural. Her standing on a rock on one foot like a flamenco.'

Jay deflated back into his slumped, spilled-stomach posture.

'No, mum, I'm not seeing anyone.' He couldn't help himself. 'And you mean *flamingo*.'

She pulled down her lip, revealing her yellowing lower teeth, as she assessed him once more.

'Well, that's a shame. You deserve somebody special. You've got nice blue eyes. Like your dad.'

Jay allowed himself to look over to the empty chair.

'Isn't that right?' she asked unnecessarily, fingers fiddling once again with her sleeves.

Jay realised his right leg was bouncing up and down. He quickly stood up and walked over to put his plate in the sink.

'Been a while since you and Katie broke up…'

'I guess.' He turned on the cold tap.

For a while there was only the sound of rushing water. He wondered what his mum was thinking. If her mind, like his, had filled with memories of his father's funeral eight months ago. Perhaps she was thinking about Cherie delivering the eulogy at the last minute as Jay, crumpled speech in his pocket, locked himself in the church bathroom, his right leg tremoring up and down, up and down.

Cherie's voice had rung out from the pulpit, so crisp and confident.

Dad wasn't a spiritual man but he was a good, kind, loyal man.

She'd sounded like she really meant it. So much so that Jay had to turn on the tap to block out the rest. He'd looked at his hands laying uselessly on top of his black M&S trousers as he forced each breath deeper and deeper into the pits

of his lungs, trying to convince himself he was fine. But still his leg bounced. When the service was over and he'd finally emerged, eyes stuck to the floor, his mum was there in the church lobby waiting for him.

'Don't worry, darling.' She'd taken hold of his arm and given him a small smile he didn't deserve. 'I've got an iffy tummy today as well.' They headed to the exit where Cherie and her then boyfriend, a goateed bass guitarist named Cliff, were waiting by the car. 'Steer clear of Aunty Myla's sausage casserole at the wake.'

The kitchen tap continued to pour.

'Your Katie had such funny hair, didn't she?' His mum had to raise her voice to be heard over the running water. 'Too red. Not real red. Red like a fire truck. Like ketchup.'

There was more silence between them. More loud water splurts.

Jay looked at his plate in the sink. In four decades, his mother had never once let him clear the table. She was always hovering, invasively helpful. But right now, all her helpfulness seemed to have drained away. Her empty eyes fixed on a discoloured patch on the cream kitchen wall.

'You're not lonely are you, Jay?' she asked.

He stared at the water gushing from the tap. She stared at the stain on the wall.

'What do you get up to stuck in that pokey little flat?'

Still the water propelled out. Still the stain captivated.

'You ever build that model ship you were collecting parts for?'

Water-boarded mustard glooped off Jay's plate and slopped next to the plughole.

'It was nice you did that, Jay. Nice you had a hobby.'

Jay unlatched himself from his locked-in daze. He turned

off the tap and turned around. He took in the kitchen that, on so many occasions, had housed not just the four of them but also aunts, uncles, cousins, friends, neighbours. For the last eight months he'd determinedly avoided having to step inside. He'd always arranged to meet his mother for lunch at cafés or claimed to have non-existent plans when dropping her home after her library volunteering. Now, here he was, finally back, with his mother at the kitchen table, looking tired and small, like a faded photograph curling in on itself.

'I finished the ship ages ago.' He cleared his throat. 'I'll send you a picture.'

'I'd like that,' she said, her eyes finally leaving the stain on the wall and meeting his. 'You know…' One finger slowly stroked her wedding ring. 'I think his name was Hoyt.'

'Sorry?'

'Yeah, that's it.' Her face brightened. 'Hoyt. Cherie's fella. The yoga teacher.'

Jay dragged his hands across his face as yet another conversation with his mother boomeranged back to nothing.

'Cherie sent me a flyer for his class. I've got it round here somewhere.'

She hoisted herself up and started pulling out tat from a kitchen drawer.

'Maybe Cherie could ask if Hoyt knows any yoga classes you'd enjoy. You might meet someone there, Jay.'

'Who?' He despaired. 'Courteney Cox's step-sister's second cousin?'

The worktop was scattered with the drawer's contents – opened envelopes, receipts, instruction manuals, letters dated five, ten years ago.

'Courteney who?'

Gas bills. Shopping lists. *That's Life!* magazines. A flyer for

a chippie that had long burned down.

'Nobody.' Jay sighed. 'I'm fine, Mum. You don't need to worry about me.'

She pulled something from the drawer that made her freeze.

'What is it?' Jay moved towards her. 'Mum?'

She was holding a grubby, faded polaroid. Decades old. Buried for years in a dusty drawer underneath *Vote Labour* leaflets for the 1997 election. She let him gently take it from her hand so he could look more closely.

It featured all the family sitting around the kitchen table for Cherie's birthday. Each of them clad in garish '90s outfits. His mother sported plentiful, back-combed hair. His sister, in her awkward, pre-teen, baby-fat phase, leaned self-consciously over a cake, the candles making the silver of her braces gleam. Jay was there too, a tall, skinny sixteen-year-old in a too-big football shirt. He was resting against the wall, arms folded, mouth half-open, seemingly mid-sentence. His dad sat in his chair at the table, only half in frame. The side-profile showed off his imposing nose, thick moustache and big stomach. He was looking directly at birthday girl Cherie with a beaming, bright smile.

'Blast from the past,' Jay said, lacking commitment.

His mother looked up and pointed at the wall, at the brown patch she'd stared at earlier. 'That tea stain's not in the photograph,' was all she said.

Jay also looked at the stain on the cream kitchen wall. Considered all its different flecks and shades.

She pointed to the same spot, stainless, in the picture. 'It must have got dirtied after. Your father always said he'd paint over it. Never got around to it in twenty-odd years. Mind you, it'd have been a sight to see if he'd tried to do it at the end.'

There was a silence. Jay's right leg bounced once, twice before he got it under control.

'He wasn't always the best to you, was he?' She asked in a small voice.

Jay pressed his tongue to the bottom of his mouth. He shook his head. They both looked at the large man in the photograph, sitting back in his chair, almost, but not quite, slipping out of the frame's edge.

'Fathers of boys… it's not always easy.' She said it so simply, so neatly, like the memory that had taken a hold of her was now being folded away like freshly ironed clothes. 'He tried his best.'

Jay looked at the stain. The photo. His mum – already resuming her little performance, rifling through her crap-filled drawers. He thought of his sister's words at the funeral. Of his father in the hospital, how he'd sat with him, watching him stubbornly bringing a cup of tea up to his lips as his broken body shook beyond his control. Even when the warm tea spilled over the edges and scalded his trembling hands, he'd kept trying to take a sip. Jay had stepped in at that point and held the cup to his father's mouth as he took a tentative sip, both of them looking anywhere but each other's eyes.

Then, Jay thought of himself sitting in that church toilet with his pathetic, tremoring leg.

'Dad threw a mug of scalding tea straight at my head, Mum,' Jay said, bluntly, loudly, making her jump. 'I remember. And I know you remember as well. But I don't remember why. Do you?'

His mum's eyes pulsed wide. She reached forward to take the polaroid out of his hand but he gripped it tighter.

'Bad school report? Sloppy appearance? A look on my face that I didn't know how to wipe off?'

She turned away from him.

'At least I ducked in time.' He added, getting louder. 'Eh? At least I was good at that.'

'He tried his best,' she repeated.

Jay let out a scathing laugh.

'His best?' He felt his whole body needling with decades of frustration. 'Do you even know the last conversation I had with Katie with the fire-engine-red hair who owns a dog called Penelope? It was about children. About how *she* wanted them but *I* didn't because... well, what if that was my best as well?'

Jay shot his hands helplessly back towards the stain, then shrugged and shook his head. His mother's shoulders wilted.

'He – '

'Don't, Mum. Just don't.'

She turned back towards him and Jay felt his anger stutter. The picture in his hand became just a picture again, a piece of the past, something that he could stuff back in a drawer and try to forget. He thought of his mum, small and alone, night after night, waiting for Cherie or him to call. Waiting for them to tell her some precious scrap of nothing about their lives.

'I'll paint over the stain, Mum,' he said, scratching his neck even though there was no itch. 'I'll come back with the right stuff and sort it for you. Next weekend.'

'No, no,' she said, wafting her hand through the air, and he saw, for the first time, her struggling to flicker herself back into fine. 'I mean, if you want to... But don't do it for me.'

For a second, they both stood still on the ancient kitchen tiles like the last two domino pieces to tumble. The polaroid remained in Jay's hand. Slowly, he sat down and placed

it in the middle of the kitchen table.

'You know, I was certain his name was Hoyt, but now I'm not so sure.' She looked at him with hope in her eyes that he might, once again, play along. 'Maybe it was Henrik. Or Humphrey.'

He sucked in a breath.

'Here, Mum…' After a few seconds of silence, he decided to smile. To make his presence, his voice, his face, everything, a big, bright distraction. 'Let's watch that movie.'

He tucked the polaroid into his pocket.

'Watch what movie?'

'The Uma Thurman one. *The Truth About Cats And Dogs*. I'll rent it for us.'

She looked at him with uncertainty.

'Come on, you'll like it. Plus, you can find out more about your future son-in-law's famous cousin.'

Her mouth gawped wide in horror.

'Jay, don't you get me into trouble! I can't be getting on the wrong side of them celebrities. I can't have you spreading their private business around.'

He leaned back in his chair. Looked up expectantly.

'Should I put it on? The movie?'

'Go on then.' She smiled at him, eyes grateful and gleaming. 'Anything's better than her in those silly yellow pyjamas.'

Just Be Yourself

<u>*Love Yacht Season 5 Application Form*</u>

Name: Callie MacNeil *Age:* 23
Job: Part-Time Retail Assistant

Please write a dating profile for yourself.

How about…

Bottle blonde seeks showmance. Fundamentally unlovable due to deep-rooted distrust of anybody stupid enough to fall in love. Willing to engage in sexually gratifying relationship with minimal emotional engagement (as long as it benefits me).

Too honest?

How long have you been single?

I avoid referring to any man I'm sleeping with as 'my boyfriend'. I always leave before daylight and only reply to their texts between the hours of one and three am.

Describe your healthiest and happiest relationship.

Probably my fifty-three-day romance with Hamish Finn when we were ten. We spoke directly on the seventh, nineteenth and thirty-third days. He gave me a mermaid pendant from a Christmas cracker. I still have it stashed somewhere in my jewellery box.

Have you ever been in love?

No.

Engaged?
No.

Married?
Hell no.

Do you already have a claim to fame?
Does appearing in an advertising campaign for my friend's uncle's used-car business count? I also once auditioned for a low-budget horror film. I overheard the casting agent telling his colleague: 'She's very expressive… she'll wrinkle young.' I can happily confirm that since then I've mastered my expressionless, dead-inside look but, if the *Love Yacht* producers are still worried about my long-dormant laughter lines, I'll happily botox my face into a terrifying paralysis-mask.

I mean, I wasn't even the best performer in my family. My brother was a sensational Rolf the Nazi in our school's production of *The Sound Of Music*. (I was an underwhelming Nun No.4.) I always thought, with his charm and my shamelessness, we could have ruled the world. It's so unfortunate his life was derailed by his poorly thought through decision to fall in love.

Tell us about your biggest break up.
I ended my last official relationship by simply turning off my phone. It seemed the easiest way to communicate my desire to be miserable and alone. I didn't have it in me to send a text saying 'it's not you, it's me (and my crippling inability to cope with grief)'. Of course, my ex still turned up at my brother's funeral doing this insufferable good-guy-offering-moral-support act. I should have been nicer to him at the wake, but that seemed too vulnerable/co-dependant/risky.

Are your family supportive of your decision to apply for Love Yacht?

They just want to see me settled and happy.

So, no.

Although… when we were growing up, my brother was pretty supportive of my attention-seeking endeavours. He always told me, 'Callie, just be yourself and they'll *love* you.' I remember him cheering me on when I entered the local beauty pageant (my talent was my impression of Janice from *Friends*). He'd say I was brave for putting myself out there. Let me tell you, when you're this innately obnoxious and self-aggrandizing, nothing you do takes bravery.

For example, I was unfazed by our bored, half-asleep audience for *The Sound of Music*, while my brother was *so* nervous. He said that he wished he was more like me. He didn't want to care what people thought about him. But that was his problem. He cared too much. Felt everything.

I often think about him saying that. Because, if he had been more like me, he'd probably still be alive. But, then, well, he'd also be more like me.

Do you have any medical concerns/questions we need to know about?

I probably should tell you about the anti-depressants that give my handbag, when shaken, a distinctive rattle. I really should start taking those more regularly.

Do you agree to undergo psychological screening to confirm you are mentally suitable for the show?

I mean, what is the 'mentally suitable' way to function on national television? Is it to flutter your eyelashes at any man who acknowledges your existence? Perhaps the 'mentally suitable' candidate is somebody who won't care when

their social media is flooded with thousands of messages calling them an 'ugly, plastic loser'? Somebody who can deal with their parents' shame when their ex uploads their grainy, mobile-phone sex tape? Somebody whose ego can cope with the inevitable and very public dissolution of their relationship and happiness?

Perhaps your 'mentally suitable' candidate is someone who didn't cry when they attended their 22-year-old brother's funeral. Someone who looked blankly at his coffin with the image of his heart, defunct and decomposing, lodged in their mind. Someone who is both shameless and numb. Who can tell themselves 'this dead-brother-bit will make a great reality TV sob-story one day' and only feel a little bit sick inside.

Describe your perfect love story.

Girl meets boy. Girl marries boy. Girl leaves boy. Boy slits wrists. You know, that old classic?

My brother was just 22. He'd been married for eight months when she left him. They were both so young. He placed his value and sense of worth in the hands of other people and – what a surprise – it went wrong.

The note he left on the kitchen counter was addressed only to her; his so-called wife. She was backpacking around America with girlfriends when my parents finally managed to get hold of her. Apparently, she went quiet for a while then she said she couldn't afford the flight back for the funeral. My parents sent her the money. She had a nice tan at the service.

Have you ever had your heart broken?

After his wife left him, when it was clear my brother was suffering, I took him out one night to try to cheer him up.

We ended up in a club. I was trying anything to haul him back from the brink and I thought all he needed was just to let loose a little. I remember, as the night progressed and we drank more and more, a look slowly crawled across his face. For the first time in weeks, there was an expression, an existence within him. I smiled at him; a really stupid, gormless grin. And his lifeless eyes revved a little, but, I realised too late, this look on his face wasn't what I'd thought. He wasn't happy. He was disgusted.

'You think you're special, Callie. But you're not. You're just like everybody else in here. Pointless. And embarrassing. And totally alone.'

I let him go. I watched him walk out, shaking his head at who he'd finally realised his little sister was. But I stayed out that night. I drank and danced with some people – some strangers – who, for a few hours, helped me ignore the nothingness inside.

I only saw my brother one more time after that. We pretended that night out had never happened and made stilted conversation across the dining-room table as our mum served us home-cooked food. Somehow, seeing the stark emptiness back on his face that night was even more heart-breaking than his look of disgust.

Do you have any connections to Love Yacht that you need to declare?

Well, my dead brother and his estranged wife were the runners-up on Season 1. Ring any bells? Somebody from production sent flowers to the funeral. Oh, and you posted that *lovely* solitary condolence tweet.

You have 30 seconds to convince us you are the Love Yacht contestant of our dreams... what do you say?

Go on, let me fashion some dental floss into a bikini, glue on some polyester hair extensions and come on your stupid show. Let me give the one performance my brother never could: the performance of being OK when deep down everything that makes sense, everything that makes you feel purposeful and warm, is draining, and draining fast. I give that performance every single day. Why not add some cameras?

Everybody's Favourite '90s Cult Sci-Fi TV Series Sidekick

I have spent the last 72 minutes willing Luke Ryan's bladder to reach capacity. I'm watching him slowly sip his soft drink as I stand in the corner of his autograph stand, ready to spring into action at any second. That's because I am taking the privilege and responsibility of stewarding *the* Luke Ryan to and from the toilets at his *ComicClash* signing session very seriously. On my arrival this morning I completed two practice runs of the route and flashed my ID lanyard to security so quickly that I gave myself a paper cut. This is not, I should admit, solely in the name of duty, for it is my great hope that during these chaperoned walks to the toilet, Luke Ryan and I are going to become lifelong best friends. Or, at the very least, I am going to get myself one *awesome* selfie.

TOILET BREAK 1

'Another demon that wants to eat children's souls? Is the vegan movement ever going to hit hell?'
– Ramsay Hunter, *Phantom X*, Season 3 Ep 1

Luke puffs out his cheeks. His eyes seem a little disorientated as he shakes his wrist.

'Intense,' he says, looking towards but through me. The queue of expectant fans, all clutching memorabilia emblazoned with his face, crane their necks to see why he's suddenly left his seat.

'This way, please.' My voice creaks out and my face blotches with embarrassment. Not the best start. Although, it's fitting to be thrust back into puberty in the presence of my childhood hero. Luke Ryan was the inspiration behind my old frosted tips hairstyle and the reason I owned a wardrobe of oversized skater clothes even though I was – and still am – physically unable to remain upright on a skateboard.

I hold the door open, leading him into the venue's airport-hangar-sized backstage area. As we travel down a lengthy corridor, the repetitive thud of his boots magnifies in the vast space. My heart seems to thump just as loudly. I flash my neon-yellow pass at a security guard and receive a puzzled look, realising too late that he's a janitor. Still, the all-access pass emboldens me, as does Luke by my side. I imagine we are striding to our next mission in slow motion as a motivational orchestration underscores the action. *Operation Toilet.*

'This is *long*,' Luke's exasperated voice jolts me out of my fantasy.

'Yeah.' A lengthy silence hangs between us. 'It's long.'

Luke Ryan is talking to me. Luke Ryan, a.k.a. Ramsay Hunter, a.k.a. everyone's favourite sidekick on the '90s cult sci-fi TV show *Phantom X*. I never missed an episode of the adventures of Phantasia, an ancient ghost warrior stuck in a high-school cheerleader's body. I've spent my entire life telling people – from the kids who mocked my *Phantom X* school bag to my family questioning why I still collect the action figures – that 'it's a *much* deeper show than it sounds'. And it's true. *Phantom X* is post-modern televisual art.

'There's not a closer bathroom?' He asks.

'No,' I reply, my chest tightening. 'I'm really sorry.'

Another silence. I clear my throat but the words still feel sticky.

'It's just thirty more seconds or so – '

'Who's got that booth?' Luke jerks his head at a door leading back into the convention hall. 'That's a prime position.'

'Uh… I think that's where Cole Sprouse is set up.'

He gives me a blank look. Up close, I can see the grey in his stubble and the wrinkles around his eyes. I guess they put a lot of makeup on twenty-somethings playing teenagers on TV. Although, to be fair, he's nearing forty now.

'From *Riverdale*,' I explain.

He lets out a short laugh without smiling. I twist my lanyard strap tightly around my finger.

'Do you watch *Riverdale*?' I ask.

I get the same laugh again.

When we reach the bathroom, he gives me one final bemused look before he goes inside.

On the walk back, Luke keeps rubbing his eyes and rolling his shoulders. I guess he needs to limber up before re-entering the den of sycophancy. There's no denying that conventions are full-on. Fans will enthuse, cry and cram their life story into their allocated thirty seconds. My friend Ivan still boasts about the time he got a high five from a Jabba the Hutt puppeteer.

Luke is undoubtedly one of the best stars to meet. He's been on the convention circuit for years and he's a total pro – American without being *too* American. He always hugs overwhelmed fans, applauds their costume efforts and obligingly regurgitates iconic lines. But right now, he seems disengaged.

'To be honest…' I think of the most ego-boosting thing to say without coming across like an intense mega-fan who's crafted multiple Lego versions of him. 'I think *Riverdale* is basically just a rehash of all the good things about *Phantom*

X. Everything they do, you guys did better. I mean they even had a whole alien arc with an identical resolution to Ramsay's Season 2 possessed convent sub-plot.'

I wince, feeling too much like a try-hard. But a wry smile works its way across his face.

'You really think that?'

'Yeah,' I enthuse. 'And another thing I noticed is that – '

'So, you're a fan…' He stops walking and looks down at my nametag. 'Gregor?'

I nod, my whole body feeling brighter for him saying my name.

'Listen, Gregor, can you do me a favour?' He puts his hand on my shoulder to stop me from moving and speaks in a hushed voice. 'These things can be really draining. Can you bring me a Coke to the booth?'

'Sure, no problem,' I nod a little too enthusiastically.

'And maybe ask the barman to pour a little vodka in it for me, will you?'

His hand on my shoulder now gives me an encouraging squeeze.

'I'll take another bathroom break in thirty minutes to get it off you.'

'I… I don't know if I'm allowed – '

He lets out a small chuckle.

'Sure you are. I'll be super grateful, buddy. Sign anything you want.'

'Uh…' I look around. People in the hallway don't seem to have noticed that the actor Luke Ryan and I are having a friendly, private, shoulder-squeezing chat. That he is asking me for a favour. That he just called me buddy.

'Or get a picture together. Whatever you want.'

He winks. He knows he has me.

'OK,' I say. 'Sure thing.'

'You're a great kid.' He claps my shoulder one final time. 'Actually, tell the barman to make it a double.'

TOILET BREAK 2

'I'm not scared. I'm just practising my impression of Edvard Munch's The Scream.'
– Ramsay Hunter, *Phantom X*, Season 1 Episode 12

Luke rises from the signing table and heads straight over. I look at my supervisor, who nods and opens the door. In the hallway, I hand him the double vodka I've hidden behind the blackout curtains.

'You are a legend.' He takes a gulp.

I'm already drafting my post on the *Phantom X* message boards: 'The day the LEGEND Luke Ryan called *me* a LEGEND'. I want to ask immediately for that promised picture but we're expressly forbidden from 'hassling' the talent so I need to wait until there's no one around.

Luke cricks his neck. 'Let's stretch our legs and head to the far-flung continent where they keep the bathroom.'

Drink in hand, Luke seems more at ease. He walks at a leisurely pace, chest puffed out, arms swinging.

'You from around here, Gregor?'

'Yep,' I sigh. 'Born and bred. This is my fifth year working here.'

Luke whistles.

'The first year I was mainly on the door, but last year I looked after the guy who composes the music for the *Transformers* series.'

A puff of air shoots out of Luke's nose.

'He was really nice. But it's super cool to be paired with you.'

'I'd never even heard of this town until I got booked for my first convention,' Luke interjects. 'I thought, why not? They stuff your wallet with money and, hey, I'll get to travel and experience some British culture.' He laughs to himself. 'You know where I can get any of that culture? And before you say anything, I've already done the magic stone by the river thing.'

'Yeah, it's pretty quiet around here,' I concede.

'The hotel bar's always crawling with fans. I don't want somebody asking about continuity errors while I'm flirting with the cute waitress.'

He laughs and I join in even though I'm oblivious to any and all forms of flirting. I spent two years exchanging online *Game Of Thrones* reviews with my now girlfriend before she pointed out we could actually meet in person. I'd still be stuck in the sending memes part of our courtship process otherwise.

'So, where do you go for a good drink around here?' he asks casually, as if speaking to a trusted friend.

'Um…' I try the name of somewhere my brother and his police pals always talk about. 'The Cross Keys?'

'The Cross Keys. Interesting shout, Gregor. Interesting shout. They got cable sport?'

I bluff. 'Oh sure.'

'You a sports fan?'

'I've been to the races a few times with my brother,' I say, remembering an unfortunate recent birthday debacle where I was forced to hang with the 'lads'.

'NASCAR?' Luke asks.

'Is that a greyhound?'

When we get to the bathroom, Luke's double vodka and Coke is already gone.

On the walk back, a husky voice stops us in our tracks.

'Luke?'

We turn around to see Irene Richie, a sixty-something sci-fi veteran most famous for playing a cyborg panther-woman, marching over to us. She wrestles Luke into a hug.

'Honey, have they got you in this rat race as well? God, no, get out, get out before you go as crazy as me!' She smacks his arm as he grins. 'All day long I'm signing pictures of myself thirty years younger and thirty pounds lighter. These kids don't give two hoots that I've done Shakespeare.'

'What was the part? Lady Macbeth?' Luke asks with a wink. 'Not much acting required there, Irene, right?'

She playfully whacks him again.

'Now I couldn't land an audition to play her grandmother. It's my elbows.' She thrusts them into his face. 'They look like elephant hide, gives the game away. But, enough about me, honey, how are you? Are you sleeping? You don't look good.'

Luke's unhappy laugh returns, accompanied by flat, disconnected eyes.

'These events aren't so bad, Irene. I've got a Q and A in a bit. They can be fun.'

She pulls a face and waves her bangled arms.

'Oh god, the Q and As. I never know what they're on about with the questions about the spells and the amulets and the metaphorical-thematical-spiritual-subtext-of-the-whatever. Who cares? These people need a hobby, am I right? Hey, how's Jeanie?'

Luke hesitates.

'She's OK.'

If there was an inch of give left in Irene's yanked tight face, her eyebrows would have shot skyward with scepticism.

'No, we, uh, yeah, we're not really… together anymore.'

Luke runs his hands distractedly through his hair. 'I don't know why I'm being weird – it's a known thing. It's not entirely acrimonious but it's also… not not.' He scuffs his feet along the floor.

Irene looks over to me expectantly then clocks the bright lanyard. I take half a step back. Her own escort had the decency to eavesdrop from a few feet away.

'Well, onto bigger and better things. Are you working?'

'Yeah. Yeah, yeah. Yeah.' He clicks his fingers as if remembering something. 'I just did an episode of *Dreadsville*.'

Luke smiles a little too earnestly. That episode aired at the end of last year.

'Well, you'll make more than ten episodes of *Dreadsville* here. This is paying for my next chin lift.' She laughs as his eyes stay stuck to the floor. 'See you around, Luke. Stay sane.'

She rattles down the hall, her escort chasing after her.

I wait for Luke but he's watching her leave. His mouth twists from side to side like he's swishing a tart-tasting mouthwash.

'Irene Richie,' he says, eventually. 'What the hell happened there? I used to tug myself off to her every night back in the day.'

I laugh even though I don't find it funny.

'Who did it for you?' Luke asks as we start walking again.

'Me?'

'Lucy Lawless? Sarah Michelle Gellar? Those Roswell chicks? Patrick Stewart? Hey, no assumptions, man.'

He laughs at my discomfort, almost inflated back to his chatty, brash best.

'I don't know…' I can feel my cheeks starting to flush. 'My brother liked Sarah Michelle… He'd only watch the show with me if she was in some kind of sportswear.'

'Sounds like my kind of guy,' Luke says casually and I feel

a surge of unease in my stomach. 'But you?'

'Scully,' I feel obliged to reply, my voice dropping to a near whisper.

He whistles his approval. 'Stern and down-to-business. Nice. Gillian Anderson, right?'

'Yeah.'

We stop, back at the entrance to the booth. Luke stares into space.

'I saw her in a Broadway play, like, last year. Tennessee Williams. Standing ovation.' His jaw clenches. 'And isn't she on like three Netflix shows?'

'Yeah.' I say. 'She's great.'

For a while he says nothing but his jaw moves from side to side like a saw cutting through wood.

'And still smoking hot, right?' His eyes flick back to me and he winks. I offer up another limp laugh.

Still, Luke doesn't go back through the door. I wonder if I should say something to him, like 'sorry your marriage has ended and you don't have Gillian Anderson's career – by the way, can I have that picture you promised?' But more subtle.

Instead, I find myself blurting out: 'You know, my brother thinks *Phantom X* is stupid.' I look down at my feet and watch them shuffling on the spot. 'He's a policeman and just watches procedural shows where he spends the whole time boasting he knows who the killer is and then kicks off when he gets it wrong.'

Luke chews on this interjection for a few seconds as I fight the urge to itch the mortification from every inch of my skin.

'Well, then I take my kind words back.' He flashes me that autograph-paper-white smile. I reply with my own more crooked offering. One of his hands claps onto my shoulder: 'Gregor, can you do me a favour?'

'A double vodka and Coke?'

'Make it two.'

TOILET BREAK 3

'I saved the world and flunked math all in one day. And after I was so careful to stake that vampire at an acute angle.'
– Ramsay Hunter, *Phantom X*, Season 2 Episode 7

'I'm stained with the tears of geeks.' Luke takes one of the drinks and nudges me. 'Just a joke.'

He starts counting on his fingers.

'So far I've had three butt grabs, four breakdowns, one personalised haiku – and *several* marriage proposals.' There's that wink again.

I give him my best smile but I'm preoccupied with what I saw on my phone while waiting at the bar for his drinks. Turns out if you google Luke Ryan, right after a relatively barren IMDB page, you'll find an article about the huge fight he and his ex-wife recently had in a hotel lobby after an American convention. Apparently, after an *'expletive-ridden verbal exchange'*, she damaged a *'glass sculpture of a gazelle'* and he ran away as the authorities arrived, so they, well, tasered him. He was *'incapacitated by electrical voltage'*. That must be the reason he has such a vacant, zombified look in his eyes in the mugshot accompanying the article.

My brother once described to me – in detail – what happens to a tasing victim. I can't help but imagine Luke handcuffed and disorientated, his jaw locked and his jeans soaked in his own urine.

The statement at the end of the online article said: *'Luke Ryan's spokesperson confirmed he was entering rehab for alcohol abuse.'*

I look at the already half-consumed drink in Luke's hand and the extra one in mine. A stone feels as though its sinking through the centre of my body.

Luke's phone rings.

'Tell me you fixed it.' He speaks in a different voice. Lower. Brisker. As we walk to the bathroom, he listens intently, only making intermittent 'uhuh' and 'okay' noises. 'It's disappointing,' he says suddenly, voice more irritable. I slow down to give him some privacy.

Once he's inside the bathroom, I can still hear him talking on the phone. I stand further away but his voice grows louder and angrier. Another guest, a stunt man who doubles for Vin Diesel, tries to enter the toilet. As the door opens in the man's hand, I realise Luke must have forgotten to turn the lock. I lunge forward.

'Sorry, sir, there's – '

'It's occupied, you fucking pervert.' Luke's red face appears in the crack that's been created. He wrenches the door shut.

Luke emerges from the toilet eventually. He looks down expectantly at my hands.

'Where's the other drink?' He asks sharply. He sniffs.

'I-I dropped it.' I stammer. 'That stunt guy... He-he knocked into me.'

'What a fucking asshole,' he says, shaking his head.

As we walk back, Luke seems deflated, like all that admirable assurance has slipped right out of a puncture in his face. He takes breaths so deep it's like he's trying to claw something out of the bottom of his lungs. I don't dare say anything. I'm worried if I do I'll admit to standing over a nearby bin and letting go of that cup full of vodka, my chances of ever befriending Luke Ryan likely plummeting alongside it.

We approach a security guard who has newly taken up a post on our route. He puts his hand out, indicating he wants to see our accreditation. I quickly produce my pass but he points at Luke.

'Where's yours?'

'He's a guest,' I interject. 'He's with me.'

The security guard, a tall guy in his forties with a crew cut and double chin, shrugs. 'He needs a pass.'

Luke laughs bitterly. I try infusing my eyes with the urgent message that now *really* isn't the time.

'I'm on the posters, buddy,' he says.

'I need to see your pass.'

'I'm *on* the posters.' Luke repeats, this time patronisingly slowly. Now is not the time to point out he didn't make this year's poster cut.

'He's from *Phantom X*.' I employ a hopelessly upbeat inflection in an attempt to detract from Luke's aggression.

'Phantom what?' The security guard pulls a face and my insides clench even tighter.

'Look, asshole,' Luke steps forward and I breathe so sharply into my contracted muscles that it hurts, 'I could really do without some pathetic nobody trying to feel good about his pointless little job.'

The guard's entire frame swells as he also steps forward so the two men are now only inches apart. My heart hammers in my chest and I experience the horror of sudden, overpowering flop-sweat. I need to fix things fast before this escalates into a fist-fight, the police are called and my brother is tasering my childhood hero into a urine-soaked puddle on the floor.

Luke's *Phantom X* character Ramsay didn't have any superpowers but that didn't stop him from stepping up to do the right thing again and again. So, I straighten my posture

and cock one eyebrow upwards, just like Luke/Ramsay did on the show.

'Look,' I point to the fine print on the back of my laminate. 'You don't need to get your reading glasses. It says with this pass I can escort anyone.' My intonation has changed and a slight American twang creeps into my words. 'And an escort never leaves an escortee unescorted so… if you'll excuse us, I have some urgent escorting to do.'

The guard looks bemused by my sudden character-switch. I take advantage of the momentary confusion and step forward. He allows us past.

'Thank fuck,' Luke mutters under his breath.

As we arrive back at his door, I want to both throw up and stage a victory dance, but Luke's face remains set in a scowl. He takes a deep, lung-scraping breath.

'This job,' he mutters, opening the door just a sliver, watching the queue of people waiting expectantly for his return. He closes it. I almost groan. I just want him to go back inside. Turn on the fan favourite act again. Leave me so I can reapply some extra-strength deodorant. 'You know…' He looks caught in two minds, his eyes everywhere except on me. 'There was an online petition for me to play the Green Lantern.'

I blink, processing his words.

'Did you sign it?' He asks. I don't know why but the vulnerability in his voice makes me feel uneasy. Now, my eyes avoid his.

'Yes,' I finally say. It's true. I did. Nine years ago.

He smiles, gratefully. But then, the smile disappears and he shakes his head.

I try again. 'I think you'd have been a great Green La-'

'I turned down a part in a really cool play to attend this convention.'

'Oh.'

'It was a really good opportunity to remind people that I'm more than just ghosts and high schools and stupid, sarcastic quips. But,' he grimaces, 'conventions pay more. This pays for my divorce. For my house. For… everything.'

'That must have been a tough decision,' I offer, hoping it's the right thing to say.

'Sure, make bad money doing a job I love or make lots of money reliving past glories, answering the same questions over and over.' He chews the side of his lip. 'That was my agent earlier on the phone.'

I start to sweat again. When I said I wanted Luke Ryan and I to form an unbreakable bond, I meant by playing PlayStation games and watching movie marathons, not by supporting him through an emotional breakdown in a hallway.

'He can't even get me an audition to play a lawyer in the next Marvel movie. An *audition*.'

'That's crazy,' I say in a quiet voice. Luke takes a long inhale, holding the breath for just a fraction too long. He nods to himself, as if vehemently agreeing with his own thoughts.

'Are you a loner, Gregor?' Suddenly he is very direct; his voice, his eyes, his energy. 'You love all this stuff, the show, the character, me… because you're a loner, right?'

'Uh…'

'Because that's what the show's all about, isn't it? The outsiders kicking ass and proving – what? – they're worth something?'

'It was a great show…'

'All of these people here today. To see me. They're loners too.' He says it with real conviction, like he *wants* it, *needs* it to be true. He nods assertively one final time. 'I'm a loner

too.' He doesn't seem to notice that I hadn't answered. 'It's the only way to be. Find your comforts outside of the human fucking race, I tell you that. Other people only ever disappoint.'

I watch him for a while just standing there, grappling with the challenge of being *the* Luke Ryan. Perhaps I owe him more than bar service and ego-fluffing. Because the truth is, yeah, I was a loner when I was younger. Kids at school made fun of me when I copied Luke's hairstyle. My brother ridiculed my *Phantom X* lunchbox and paid me £10 to tell his friends I was adopted. When I broke my nose failing to land yet another skateboard jump it was just an opportunity for everybody to mock me.

I shift my weight and clear my throat.

'I don't think I'm a loner.' It's the last vestige of confidence I currently have strength for. Luke frowns. 'I have some great friends now, some I met working here. I have a super-cool, funny girlfriend.' I smile sympathetically at him and his entire body bristles. 'And if people don't see that I'm happy with who I am then they can just leave me alone.'

A hard flint-like quality enters Luke's eyes.

'People?' He asks. 'Me?' The edge in his eye now enters his voice. 'Your cop brother?'

'Just people,' I say, but I imagine myself holding a taser and my brother, all those bullies, even *the* Luke Ryan crumpling before me into a heap on the floor.

For a long time, Luke just looks at me, long and hard, with widened, blood-shot eyes and a swerving jaw. I stay calm, keep my face very still and just imagine the voltage.

As if suddenly aware of his own intensity, Luke laughs and his body snaps into an attempt at casualness.

'Fuck! Whatever. God, why am I being so maudlin?' He shakes his head and continues to laugh, loudly and

mechanically, back to playing the well-practiced part of the actor who was once a well-loved sci-fi '90s TV series sidekick. 'I get to come here and be god of the nerds and I'm throwing a pity party in the hallway with a freaking fanboy.' I don't react. I let him say whatever he needs to say. 'You know, I bet even Daniel Day Lewis sometimes wishes he'd done a sci-fi show.'

He winks at me but when my face doesn't change, he sighs, shifts his eyes from side to side and drops the act once again.

'Thanks for dealing with that security jerk, Gregor. You've got a pair on you.'

I smile and so does he. My camera phone is in my pocket. I could finally ask for that photo. But I hesitate. Wonder who I'd actually be getting the picture for.

The door opens and my supervisor appears. 'Everything alright?' She shoots a glare at me. 'You ready to finish signing, Mr Ryan? We've only got five minutes before your Q and A.'

He follows her through the door but then he stops and turns back. My hand has already let go of the phone in my pocket.

'Hey, buddy. Do you mind getting me a – '

'Mr Ryan?' This time even the supervisor sounds impatient with him. 'We're *really* tight on time.'

He shakes his head. Turns away.

'Never mind.'

He steps through the door and the cheers rise.

Eulogy for a Bastard

I am here today to say something tortured and trite. To ugly cry and make you all feel uncomfortable, or perhaps I'll not cry enough and that will make you feel uncomfortable instead. I'm here to make a dead person sound like every other dead person. You know: 'beloved'. I'll probably end up saying inane, obsequious things like: 'I can never express the enormity of the hole Stef leaves behind' or 'he was a kind, gentle spirit'. And I'll definitely say: 'He lived life to the full'. You know, before his body detonated unceremoniously at thirty-nine.

Yep. It's going to be a struggle to communicate who Stef was. To me. To others. All those many, many others.

I often find myself re-reading his last text to me.

'Can u pic up cat liter. i 4got.'

No x. Poor spelling. And I didn't even reply.

For Stef, there was no dignified, profound, clean end. Just a red clot, tracing a path towards the off-switch in his brain. Then: bloop. No gasp, no fight, no fear. No chance to right wrongs. To erase incriminating photos. There was a person. Then there was just a body. Functionless bones, muscle and skin laying on the cold tiles of our bathroom floor. His unwashed gym clothes next to him, his awful country music still playing from the speakers and his mobile phone just pinging away.

Stef once told me that when he was eleven and his mother was in hospital having her breasts gutted from her body, he snuck his first dirty magazine home. Said he panicked, didn't look at it, stashed it away. Then, the night she was

finally allowed back home, he looked at her from across the landing as she was propped up in bed with a drained, grey face and he didn't go in. Instead, he went to his room and masturbated over and over to page after page of luscious, blubbery breasts.

He was crying when he told me about that. Naked in our bed, ashamed of his soft, pink penis. That was unusual. All of it. The crying, the limp dick, the emotional incontinence about troubling sexual episodes in his childhood. I was pretty repulsed but I didn't let on. I simply stroked his back and listened to him weep for his dead mother and her scarred, hollow chest.

So, I've told that story today.

Not the story about how he volunteered with Alzheimer's sufferers for a school project and let that old soldier think he was his brother. Not the story about how he jumped into that filthy canal to rescue that woman who'd fallen in. And absolutely not the story about him travelling through the night on Christmas Eve just so I didn't have to spend Christmas Day alone.

When I found Stef naked on the bathroom floor, there was a moment – just a moment – when I looked away from his glassy eyes and twisted body and watched the soap suds slip down the shower wall instead. I reached out my hand and slowly squished them dry. I thought about nothing. Convinced myself the world was just me and a blank, wiped wall. Then, the paramedics covered him in a white sheet and he was swallowed up so completely by the efficiency of death. I tidied up his clothes, turned off his music, fed the cat. Then I picked up his phone and read the messages.

You see, it turns out, death isn't neat. Death is messy and raw. It's a sheet ripped right off and a body cracked open. Death is stitches and gashes and slices. Death is time to find

the problems, time to expose the insides.

So, I read about his endless betrayals, his embarrassingly unsatiated desire to be with others. I read how he'd refer to me as 'The Exhaustion' – kind of poetic, right? – when he was discussing his many affairs with his friends. I read every single painful, twisted word.

Stef found fidelity *quite* the inconvenience.

When the ambulance crew were ready to take him away, I looked down at the pathetic shape of my partner, vacated and vulnerable, somewhere yet nowhere underneath that white cloth, and, still, all I wanted was to keep him. For one final night, I could hold him in my bed, peel back the covering, split him open and crawl inside.

A few years ago, his old school friend got in contact, said he wanted to buy me a coffee. Me. Not Stef. This guy sat across from me, sunken and ashamed, as he talked and talked. Wanted me to know how he'd been to therapy and was 'striving to be a better man' so he just *had* to tell me every detail of this holiday that he and Stef had been on in their twenties. They had driven around Italy, permanently drunk and characteristically reckless. There were dares after dares. Nothing was off limits. Screw that girl. Steal that horse. Do a runner from the most expensive restaurant. And, quite often, start a fight and then laugh as their victim bolted in a panic. One night, Stef dared this friend to square up to a skinny, young Italian who surprised them by standing up for himself. Next thing, they were speeding off in their car as police sirens approached and the Italian man lay very still on the ground, blood running from his nose.

'I see that man's face when I sleep. Does Stef?'

I paid for the coffees and left. I never asked. But once or twice I looked over at Stef while he was sleeping and wondered if a nightmare might be raging inside. Perhaps, deep

down, he tormented himself about who he was and what he'd done. Perhaps the bouts of rage and shame felt all-consuming, clogging up his insides just like that blood clot that would one day snatch him away. Perhaps he muttered in his sleep at night because his dead mother lurked in the corners of his subconscious and told him how she'd waited for him to visit her sick bed as the world began to dim.

So, I guess I was… what… complicit in Stef's cuntiness? Wilfully ignorant? Can I really stand here and condemn him – stamp my feet that I wasn't enough for him? Because… what? Because he was bad? Bad to me. Bad to you. And you. To be honest he was fucking awful to most of you. And I knew. Most of it. I *enjoyed* it. It was part of the reason I liked him, that I loved him. I was thrilled by him and his bad, careless, pig-headed behaviour. I was delighted to join in with his little escapades, his ego-trips, his disregard for anyone else. It was exhilarating to cling to his side as he took command of a room, for better or worse, as he lasered into his victim and unleashed his wrath. Just because. Because he could. It was brilliant. Until, it wasn't.

So, a bad person who did bad things has died. And still I stand in our shower and wish those soap suds were still there, clinging to the wall. Those suds were his sweat, his dirt, his filthy, sneaky, little particles of bacteria. And, yes, I think about the bad stuff. About him climbing into bed with me after spending the night fucking Carole Brightman after the office Christmas party. By the way, hi Carole – thanks so much for paying your respects today.

I think about things like that all the time. And, still, I sit at night on our sofa sniffing his whisky bottle, listening to his terrible country music, dragging a string along the ground for his stupid old cat. I carry on his donations to the breast cancer charity and I watch *The Shawshank Redemption* over

and over, waiting to hear his voice quote every line.

I have to remember both versions of him.

Because, well, as is evident from this eulogy, I am a bad person as well. But sharing this with you, ruining whatever delusion of decency you had constructed about Stef the man – now Stef the corpse – this *has* to be the last bad thing I do.

Marilyn Monroe Lets the Livestock In

'Norma Jean used to stand by the [cow's] pen and just stare at her, remarking at how pretty she was… Then the torrential rain came one night… and [Norma Jean] was going to bring her in the house. After much conversation about the matter, [her husband] convinced her that she really belonged in her pen.'

– *Marilyn Monroe: Private and Undisclosed*, Michelle Morgan

When her husband tells her no, you can't invite the wet, bedraggled cow caught in the rainstorm into the house overnight, Norma Jean kicks him out. She's had enough – why are decisions something other people always get to make?

So, she pours herself a bourbon and listens to his cursing as his truck drives down the dirt track to his mother's. Then, she swings open the front door and gently clucks her tongue. Slowly, the creature trots its way inside.

There, in her small, floral-wallpapered hallway, beauty and beast hover, uncertain. Norma Jean eyes the animal's fluorescent ear-tag, runs a nervous hand through her brunette coils, jokes about liking its earring. The animal shivers, doubt deep in its black beaded eyes. She knows it questions her kindness, not believing that comfort can ever last for long. Still, she reaches out her hand towards its soaked, bulky body. She finds that she wants it to wince. To stop being so trusting, naïve and kind.

Don't be that foster child smiling at the adult they think will always be around.

Don't be that sixteen-year-old girl marrying the man she

barely knows.

Don't be that obliging woman closing the door during another 'meeting' with the boss.

'It's good to be afraid,' she says to the cow in a soothing, whispered voice. 'Take your time to really get to know me.'

Norma Jean gives the cow some space. Lets the water evaporate from its body beside the glow of her fireplace. She stands by her kitchen window watching rain lash down like strikes of a palm. She finishes her drink and wonders where she can buy some hay.

Acknowledgements

Thank you so much to the publications and organisations that have published and promoted earlier versions of the stories in this collection.

Caturday – published in June 2021 in *So To Speak* Journal and nominated for Best of the Net.

The Red Dress – published in November 2022 in *Narrative Magazine.*

Dear Sophie – published in June 2020 in *X-R-A-Y Literary Magazine.*

Dead-Eyed – published in July 2021 in *Reflex Fiction.*

Silent Retreat – published in November 2021 in *Superlative Literary Journal* as the winner of the Superlative 2021 Short Story contest and shortlisted for the 2021 Bridport Prize.

All the Ways We're Hurting – published in March 2022 in *SmokeLong Quarterly.*

Every Shard, Every Speck, Every Particle – published in October 2022 in *Flash Fiction Online.*

The Scandals of Christendom – published in April 2021 in *Fugue Journal* as the winner of the 2021 Prose Contest Prize.

The Second Miss Thompson – runner-up in the 2021 *Writer Advice* Flash Fiction contest.

Anita Berber Takes Her Clothes Off – published in December 2022 in Blackwater Short Story Collection 2022 and shortlisted in their 2022 contest.

Just Be Yourself – published in April 2021 in *Drunk Monkeys.*

Everybody's Favourite '90s Cult Sci-Fi TV Series Sidekick – published in January 2021 in *Maudlin House.*

Eulogy for a Bastard – published in October 2021 in the

To Hull And Back 2021 Anthology and winner of the 2021 To Hull And Back Humorous Short Story contest.

Marilyn Monroe Lets The Livestock In – published in September 2022 in *Cleaver Magazine* and nominated for Best Microfictions.

Thank you so much to my family – parents, siblings, nieces, Scots, Greeks, Persians – for all being supportive and wonderful in their own individual ways. But particular thanks to my Mum who loves words and champions creativity. Plus, I know she will really enjoy uploading a poor-quality picture of this dedication to social media.

Thank you to everybody at Valley Press – especially Jo for believing in my writing and helping to make every story better.

Thank you to all the many people from the writing community who have shared countless insights and kindness. Nigel, Siobhan, Zoë, Vania, Robyn, Tonks, Lexi, Carinya, Khal, Helen, Sara, Gwen and many more. A special mention to Chris Rodrigues, whose positivity and general loveliness is something I will always remember.

Thank you to Richard Kelly, Nell Stevens, Francis Gilbert, Morgan Talty and Vicky Grut for, at various times over the years, being honest and generous mentors.

So many wonderful friends have been amazing cheerleaders – thank you to them all, but particularly to Ian, Ed, Nicola, Tom, Gemma and Catherine.

Thank you to Jabiz for everything.

Finally, to Hector McMillan. A teacher unlike any other. I don't remember much from accounting (!) lessons, but I do remember being valued as an individual. Anything that may be perceived as unique about me or my writing, flourished thanks to spending time with people who created environments like that.

About the Author

Emma Brankin is a writer and educator from Glasgow, Scotland with a Masters in Creative Writing and Education from Goldsmiths College, University of London. Her work has been shortlisted for the Bridport Prize's Short Story Contest. In 2021, she won the Short Story contests for *Fugue Fiction*, *To Hull and Back* and *Superlative*. Other stories have appeared in publications such as *Narrative Magazine*, *SmokeLong Quarterly* and *X-R-A-Y Literary Magazine*. She assists her cat Sabre with his burgeoning social media career where he shares book recommendations on Instagram via @sabre_reads.

CPSIA information can be obtained
at www.ICGtesting.com
Printed in the USA
LVHW031215150723
752518LV00007B/1052

9 781915 606280